A SPARROW IN THE WIND

a novel

JANET L. MANTIA

Dedicated to my mother.

Loved and deeply missed.

Not a sparrow falls to the ground

without the knowledge of our Creator.

Chapter 1

June 1975 ~ Pittsburgh, Pennsylvania

The bedsprings squealed as Sammy stared at the ceiling, unaware someone soon would be plotting his death. Not knowing how life will change, the orphan at St. Joseph's Home for Boys gazed through the open blinds in the window. As he watched the moon inch its way down through the sky, even stars set afire could not be extinguished by the darkness. Yet nothing is as it seems. The black of night could not hide the sorrow of boys, stacked in their bunks, who had neither a father nor a mother.

Sammy turned when the door swung open and Father John's long frame loomed in the doorway. Was it fate that the Headmaster of St. Joseph's School for Boys, Father John Christopher, shared the same initials as Jesus Christ? Standing in the center of the room, his cassock blended into the night with only the band of his collar providing the sole touch of white that glowed in the moonlight. Then like a shepherd tending his flock, Father John raised his hand and made the sign of the cross before easing the door shut.

Moonlight settled over the room as Sammy listened to the moan of a black crane-necked fan sitting on the bureau. Its blades cranked to a steady rhythm, trying to cool a room paneled with rough oak boards, but it sprayed only hot air across the space. With a forehead gleaming in sweat, Sammy watched as Steven Gold, nicknamed Goldy, got up from his bed. He was fourteen, the same age as Sammy, with hair the color of a new football curled tight to his head and the muscles of a man beginning to mold to his chest. His frame cast a shadow on the wall before he spoke. "I got everything, and I hope it comes tonight." Then placing a napkin on the bed, Goldy opened the wrinkled square of fabric to reveal a link of bratwurst surrounded by crusts of bread.

But Sammy sat rigid. "Shhhh … someone's coming," he said, as the night watchman shuffled down the hall. The short, well-fed watchman kept vigil and roamed the building in the dead of night, twirling a wooden club and whistling a shrill monotonous tune. Sammy listened to his whistle that sounded like a freight train pounding down a road of iron tracks. His shoulders relaxed when the piercing sound faded into the night.

Sammy pushed back the covers and swung his legs from the bed. The cuffs of his pajamas mopped the old wood floor as he lifted the sash of the window, sending a shriek of protest from its rusted hinges. Feet then traipsed across the floor as boys, some tall and lean, some short and stout, formed a line in front of the window for their escape into the backyard. When it was Sammy's turn, air breathed its way up his pajama legs, and he felt he was drifting, floating from a cloud. There were no rules tonight, no prayers to recite or beds to make. And at the moment his bare feet hit the lawn below, he was free.

With the night shrouded in an eerie stillness, the wedge of an eastern moon lit the blue-black sky. Under a cover of darkness, the moon shone silver through the trees as Sammy led the boys to a cluster of towering maples where the *creature* had always taken the food which disappeared by morning. Until tonight, no one had been brave enough to stay and see what would retrieve the meager rations. But tonight was different. Sammy felt brave enough to fight off a bear, or perhaps it would be the stray cat, with a crooked bottle-brush tail, that climbed onto their window ledge at night to sleep.

Standing under the maple tree, Sammy spread out the napkin, placing the bratwurst in the center and surrounding it with crusts of bread. With the food at the base of the tree, each boy assumed his position behind a large shrub. Watching. Waiting. But when a thorn sliced into Sammy's toe, he jerked back from the ragged bush. Balancing his weight on his heel, Sammy rocked from side to side, but stopped when he heard the rustle of leaves. He then spoke above a whisper. "Be quiet. I hear something."

In the silence there was a presence about to make itself known. Everyone was still, but ready to bolt, when a skeleton of a man appeared. The collection of bones swayed and jerked when he walked, like someone was pulling the strings of a puppet. Edging closer he appeared tall and lanky, with a knob of a head that bobbed up and down like a bird in search of food. A narrow face, covered in a patina of dirt, hung from a nest of unkempt hair. Then standing like a spindly fence rail, bathed in moonlight, he smoothed down wrinkled trousers as if grooming himself for dinner. His smell, his scent cloaked the night. It was a scent hard to describe — a foreign smell — a smell of other times and places.

Sammy was the first to emerge from behind the bush. "Who ... are you?"

The man looked up with eyes that appeared as two black stains and teeth like rows of corn cob, that glistened in the moonlight. "Name's Calvin Davis," he said, with a thick southern drawl. "Born in Memphis, Tennessee. An jess lemme say this, ya boys have it mighty good here. A warm bed. Cooked meals." The man paused a moment. "Ya know, I was an orphan once. But never had me such comfortable accommodations."

With spidery arms that bent in all directions, the man began to gnaw on the bratwurst. Then lowering his thin frame, he sat cross-legged on the ground with his long legs protruding from his sides like a grasshopper. The boys swarmed around him, intrigued by the bug-like creature of a man who slid a toothpick from his pocket and began to jab at his teeth. Sammy stared the longest. He envied the man digging bratwurst from his teeth, a man who could go anywhere and roam the countryside. It was unlike his life at St Joseph's. He was free.

The man stood, folding boney arms across his chest. "Wanna know somethin' … I travel whichever way the wind's blowin'. And with a south wind blowin', reckon I'll head to Florida. But ya gotta know jess how to jump a train. Gotta get a good start and move ya body the right direction. And don'tcha worry about puttin' out more food. May bring a fox, or mebbee a bear."

The man cocked his head back and let out a cackle, a shrill piercing sound that cut through the night. After his laughter calmed, he threw the remnants of a jacket over his shoulders. Then stomping his boots in the grass, he lurched at the boys. "Now git. Skeedadle, ya pitiful or … orfens." The man crumpled his shoulders, buckling with laughter, as everyone ran toward the window and took turns hoisting themselves back into their room.

Sammy crawled into bed and pulled the covers to his chin. Was he waking from a nightmare or entering into one? When things were unpleasant, or too painful to think about, Sammy pushed the thought from his mind and tried to convince himself it was a dream. And he wondered if it was a dream when his mother stood in a cloud of mist with her blonde hair swirling about her face. She was sobbing and spoke through her tears. 'I have to go, but an angel will come to watch over you.' She then stepped back into the mist and disappeared from his life. It was as though the world had been torn down, but the sun rose the next morning. Until her death, Sammy had never lost anything worth grieving over. People once envied the striking boy, with dark hair and eyes and the height of a man. Now they pitied him.

The pain tightened in his chest when Sammy thought of his mother standing behind the counter at Wiley's Hardware Store where she worked. She wore a smock at the store, and when she washed the blue smock, he thought of the ocean as it floated on top of the white chipped basin. Then wearing the smock, with the name of the store embroidered on the front, she mixed paint in a hundred shades and sorted nuts and bolts into plastic bins.

The owner of the store, Tom Wiley, had hair gray at the temples and a stern face, but his lips creased to a smile when he passed his mother's counter. He even bought her flowers on her birthday. Sammy dreamed one day his mother would marry Tom and they would all live on the other side of town, where big homes and bearded maples lined the sidewalks and made pools of shade on the brick streets. But his mother continued to pay rent for their apartment on Foster Street with radiators that hissed and a toilet that didn't flush; and she never married.

Maybe it was because of his mother's *special* heart. She said God gave her a special heart — one not as strong as the heart beating in his chest. He remembered the day of his mother's death as a cold, rainy day, as if the heavens were weeping. And when he came home from school, and Mrs. Olson from across the hall was there with swollen eyes, he knew it was because of his mother's special heart. He stood unable to move, and as Sammy listened to Mrs. Olson sob, everything in the apartment appeared to stand still. The clock on the wall seemed to stop ticking, its brass hands holding steady at four o'clock. The only movement was his chin quivering as he tried to hold back his tears.

Sammy thought back and remembered the car that parked in front of their apartment building after his mother died. He imagined the taxi was a yellow carriage with a queen inside who had come to rescue him. But the woman who emerged wore a stiff navy suit, and when she tried to smile her face was tense, her lips pursed. She then bundled him off and they drove toward St. Joseph's Home For Boys, bouncing along streetcar tracks carved deep into the streets. When the taxi screeched to a halt, they stepped onto a path of bricks leading to a stately residence surrounded by trees. The woman with lips of stone then rang the doorbell and left Sammy on the steps before turning to walk away.

Sammy tried to forget that day. He then laid his head on the pillow and stared into the dark at Alan, who lay in the bed beside him. But Sammy turned his head to escape the smell of urine that rose from

Alan's bed. Yet Father John said not to scold, but pray that the youngest boy at St. Joseph's Home would adjust to his new life. But it was not the smell of soiled sheets, but fear that hung in the air. Who was the drifter, the man with a southern drawl that roamed from town to town, traveling whatever way the wind was blowing? Was it a dream, or did he meet the *boogey man*? Sammy wiggled his toe where a thorn had been imbedded under his skin. The toe throbbed, and he knew tonight was not a dream. He met a man with eyes cold and black as an iron skillet.

Six Months Later

The Christmas tree in Father's John's office, dense with red bulbs, wore a garland of tinsel and flashed rows of bright-colored lights. But as Sammy waited for the Headmaster to arrive, he sat wondering why Father John had summoned him. He then turned his gaze to a framed picture on the desk and recognized the long-legged boy, with jagged-cut bangs, as Father John. He posed in front of what appeared to be his home in Ireland, a plaster-like cottage that had a sod roof. At Father John's feet sat a dog with a thin snout that looked like a sheltie, a sheep-herding dog. As he stared at the picture, Sammy thought of the boy who became a man, with kind green eyes and loved God more than anyone he knew. His thoughts were interrupted when Father John entered.

"I was about your age there," Father John said, staring down at the gold-framed picture. "And that was my dog, Flossie. What a good dog she was. Best sheep herder in Wilshem County." He paused to rustle Sammy's hair. "How are you, lad?"

"I'm fine, sir."

"I wanted to see you cause I have good news. You may have a new family by Christmas. The Swinehausers would like to adopt you ... you'll be meeting them next week. And did you know, you share the same birthday, July 4th, as Mr. Swinehauser?" Sammy stared deep into Father John's eyes. He would be leaving St. Joseph's, leaving everything he had grown accustomed to; and he was unsure, apprehensive about his new name, *Sammy Swinehauser.* He wondered if the boys at school would call him a swine, or worse yet would they call him a pig?

Sammy forced a smile. "I'm glad. We all want to have a family."

"I thought you would be happy. Now run along, or you'll be late for class."

Sitting in math class, Sammy tried to visualize his new parents, the way a mother or father tries to visualize their first-born child. He thought his father would be tall and broad-shouldered, carry a briefcase, and would wear a three piece suit. His new mother would have blonde hair that curled to her shoulders, and her purse and shoes, like the ones in the window of Gimbel's Department Store, would match the dress she wore. But when he thought of leaving his friends at St. Joseph's, sadness swept over him. Life would change, and Sammy wondered what he would become. Or what would become of him?

Sister Grace then rustled up the aisle, with the full skirt of her black habit brushing against each desk she passed. She viewed the world with piercing blue eyes, that squinted from behind wire spectacles and rattled off complex equations from memory. Now pacing in front of the chalkboard, her hands moved fast with the chalk clicking in the quiet classroom. "Do you know the square root of thirty-six?" she asked. "Do you know the square root of eight-one? Do you know ... do you know?" she repeated.

Sammy listened as Sister Grace sang an endless tune of numbers. Yet he only wanted to know about his new family. His mother once told him she named him *Samuel*, which meant he belonged to God. But since her death, he felt he belonged to no one.

Chapter 2

Walking down the hall at St. Joseph's School, Sammy blended in with students rushing to get to class. When Goldy came up beside him, they kept stride with each other, both dressed in their uniforms of black pants and white shirts. "I heard you're leaving. Anyway, I want you to have this," Goldy said, sliding a rabbit's foot into his hand. As Sammy peered down at the brown paw, clinging to a silver chain, it seemed odd for Goldy to have it — a boy who once gave an hour long presentation on the life of an earthworm — a boy who retrieved spiders in tissue and tossed them out the window.

"You know, they're supposed to bring good luck," Goldy said. For an instant, he stared down at the floor and slumped his shoulders, making his broad chest cave in, as if embarrassed by his display of emotion. Then without uttering a word, Goldy raised his head, spun his tall frame around, and disappeared into one of the classrooms.

Sammy fingered the paw of a rabbit that once ran wild in the woods, then slipped it into his pocket. He continued down the hall, but stopped when he came to Room 202, the social room reserved for meeting adoptive parents. Walking inside, he stood in front of a window painted with frost. Staring out at the frigid day, winter had tightened its grip across the landscape with a fresh mantle of snow making everything appear sterile and clean. But the pewter sky provided little light, and the weak December day appeared as a black and white photo washed over with hues of gray.

Sammy moved from the window and began to pace. He counted beige tiles on the floor, waiting for the door to swing open and Father John to arrive with his new family. As he stood staring at the door, the brass knob slowly turned and Father John entered. A man and woman followed behind. The man had a lumpy build and smoothed down the remaining strands of hair atop his head. His mustache, heavy and dense, almost walrus like, tapered to his chin. For a moment Sammy took in all the sights, all the details of a man with eyes, gray and sharp as pins, a striped tie wrung tight to his neck, and a generous girth that filled out his jacket.

Father John stood and folded thin arms across his chest. "Sammy, meet Mr. and Mrs. Swinehauser." He then stepped back and grinned. "I'll give you some time together. To get to know each other."

When Father John left, and the door slammed shut, Sammy felt alone even though he was with the man and woman who would become his parents. As if pleading with his eyes, he turned to Mrs. Swinehauser who stood tall and erect, with her hands clasped in front of her as if she were praying. She wore a coat, the color of fresh sage, had a tiny triangle of a nose, and her hair, glossy and red, veiled one side of her face. When she moved closer to Sammy, she rested her hand on his shoulder, and the scent of freshly laundered clothes surrounded her tall slender frame.

"Ahhh, just look at you," she said. "We were never blessed with children, and I know we can never take the place of your mother and father. So you can just call me Legna and this is Max. Did you know I was born in Sweden, and Legna is *Angel* spelled backwards?"

Glancing up at her, Sammy clenched his jaw and tapped his foot against the floor.

"Not shy are ya?" Max asked, his mouth hanging open in a lop-sided smile.

"Now Max, he has to get to know us." Legna then turned to Sammy. "You're growing into such a fine young man. Why don't you tell us what you boys do here."

"We go to school. Have prayer time. Sometimes we help out at the shelter. And when the weather's nice, we take field trips. Like to the zoo."

"We love to go to the zoo. Don't we, Max?"

Legna turned to Max, but he said nothing and raised his hand to conceal a yawn. Giving Max a deep stare, she moved closer to Sammy. "You know, I prayed for a son like you. And next week, you'll come home with us. We're going to be a happy family. Have ourselves a grand life!"

Max held out a large calloused hand, larger than Sammy had ever seen. "Put it here, big guy," he said, gripping his hand until it hurt. Max then lumbered to the door and held onto the brass knob, hoping to flee as fast as he entered. "It's time to go, Mother," he said. "I ate breakfast early this morning. And it's time for my lunch."

On his last day at St. Joseph's, Father John carried Sammy's possessions to the front of the building. The cardboard box, bound with layers of tape, contained a curled picture of his mother, five pairs of black pants, five white shirts, underwear, bed clothes, and some toiletries. Aside from the clothes on his back, this was all Sammy owned.

As a mean wind gnawed at the tip of his nose, Sammy watched Father John slip a gloved-hand into his pocket. "Here's something for you," he said, handing Sammy a fistful of peppermint candy. Father John moved closer, and when he wrapped his arms around Sammy, he felt he was being embraced by God. But they both looked up when a gray hearse appeared, gliding around the bend with headlights shining bright in the morning haze.

"Is there a funeral today?" Sammy asked.

"No, that's the Swinehausers. They must have brought their business car."

Staring at Max slumped over the steering wheel of the hearse, Sammy swallowed hard and squared his shoulders before he spoke. "Good … goodbye, Father John." Sammy then got into the hearse with a peeling vinyl top and edged in chrome dull as the winter day. Seated between Max and Legna, he sat staring at the coffin-like surroundings of white pleats and folds of satin, held back by gold covered buttons.

With a lingering scent of flowers filling the hearse, Legna leaned closer to Sammy. "Can't wait for you to see your room. I bought you a spread with race cars and matching drapes. Even bought you clothes for school. I got your size from Father John."

Sammy smiled at the woman who pushed waves of red hair back from her eyes — the woman with the odd name who would become his mother. As they drove from the city, a skyline of buildings was replaced by white-shouldered hills and snow covered pastures that stretched for miles. Max said little. When they stopped at a red light, he looked straight ahead and drummed the steering wheel with long square fingers. Legna broke the silence. "We live in White Chapel and Max runs the crematory business his father had. Then after his dad and mom passed away, he inherited the house he grew up in."

"Mother was a saint," Max said, "I was her little boy, and she was the only one who called me Maxim."

After Max spoke everyone grew quiet, especially Legna who seemed comfortable with silence. She then gazed out at the frozen landscape, with a sky overhead the same shade as stone boulders lining the road. Leaving the city behind, drab buildings vanished in the distance as they drove toward White Chapel where large plots of ground gave way to spacious homes with big porches and backyards that spilled into the woods.

"Our house isn't far," Legna said. "We're almost there."

After passing a vacant lot, encased by a barbed wire fence, Max turned onto Red Oak Lane. But going up the steep hill, the hearse sputtered and jerked back and forth with the speed of a lame race horse. Max tensed his jaw and pressed hard on the gas pedal. When they reached the top of the hill Max appeared relieved, as if he had coaxed an old mare across the finish line.

The hearse then veered onto a gravel road, stalled out, and came back to life before attacking the road again. When they passed a glimpse of hills, a herd of cows appeared as brown and black splotches against the snow-covered fields. As pastures faded in the distance, a sign along the road greeted anyone turning down the lane. It read:

Swinehauser's Crematory. We want to urn your business.

A level lot sprawled ahead and appeared as a vast white comforter trimmed with evergreens. In the center of the space stood a two story clapboard home with shutters in need of paint and a wooden swing suspended to the porch ceiling by a chain. On each end of the house, trees with gnarled branches rose above the roof and knotted around each other like two arms. Beyond the tangle of branches, obscure but within sight, was a building made from cinder block with a black shingled roof that sagged like a circus tent.

"Well, we're home," Legna said. "What do you think?"

When they got out of the car, Sammy glanced at the cinder block building and the white frame house surrounded by barren pastures. It appeared to be a farm without animals, and snow-covered fields without any remnants of crops. "I don't understand. How … can you have a crematory and make cream, when I don't see any cows?"

Max choked with laughter. "How come we don't have any cows? Boy, you've been at the orphanage toooo long."

For a moment Legna was silent, but then her eyes sharpened. "I'm sure Sammy's led a sheltered life at St. Joseph's. And everyone doesn't know about crematories. Especially a young boy."

Legna climbed the steps of the porch and Max followed behind. But Sammy stood glaring up at the house with his feet heavy as rocks chained to the ground. He then heard a voice say to him, *"Get away from here. Go as fast as you can. Run."* Sweat pooled on his forehead as Sammy jerked around and stared into nothing. Max shattered the silence when he shouted down from the porch. "Come on boy, what the heck ya waiting for."

Legna came down from the porch, took Sammy by the arm, and lead him to the door. "This is your new home and we're gonna be one happy family," she said.

Inside the house Sammy gazed up at high ceilings arched overhead, lace curtains the color of fresh cream, and a braided rug warming the center of the wood floor. It appeared to be the home of the grandmother Sammy wished he had. The only item his grandmother would not have was the rifle that hung on a rack above the fireplace. As his eyes continued around the room, they came to rest on a bowl with shades of the rainbow swirled through the clear glass. Sammy picked up the bowl from the table and held it against light pouring through the window.

"Hey boy! That was my mother's favorite bowl. Put it down before ya break it."

"I'm sorry," Sammy said, placing the bowl back on a scarf of starched white linen. "I ... never saw a bowl like that before."

Max could feel Legna's stare. With his lips turned into a frown, as if stitched by a needle and thread, Max laid Sammy's box of clothes down on the floor. "If you don't need me, I got work to do."

Legna nodded in agreement, and through the window, they watched Max go behind the house and into the cinder block building. She then led Sammy toward the couch. "Sit down here, I need to tell you a few things. When someone doesn't choose a regular burial, their body is reduced to ashes by high heat and kept in an urn. Or spread wherever they want their ashes spread. There's nothing wrong with being cremated. The ashes of Max's mother are in the urn on the fireplace."

Sammy stared at the silver vase on the mantel, trying to imagine the ashes inside were once a living, breathing human being.

"Another thing," Legna said, "Max is different and lives by his own rules. Gets up at six and drinks a Mr. Bud Cola for breakfast, when he's nervous he grins, and before he goes to bed, he kisses his mother's urn on the fireplace." Legna hesitated and wrung her hands. "And Max stopped going to church. Thinks we came from nothing, and when we die, we go back to nothing. I guess you can say Max believes in nothing. But don't repeat a word of this," she said, laying a finger across her lips.

Legna crossed the room and stood next to a bookcase, towering to the ceiling, with rows of books all neatly stacked. "Hope you like to read," she said.

"How many books do you have?" Sammy asked, staring at the mountain of books.

"I've never counted them, but you can read whatever you like. There's history books, biographies, and classics by Hemingway, Emerson, and Thoreau."

"Did you know that when I read a book, I read the last part of the book first? I have to know how the story ends." Sammy paused, surprised at himself for revealing that to Legna.

"But the beginning's the most important part. You have to know how the story begins, so you understand how it ends," she said.

Legna then led Sammy down a hallway, covered with somber printed wallpaper, to a spacious knotty pine kitchen. The room had a clean woodsy smell; and at the far end of the kitchen, tucked in the corner, sat a typewriter on a small wood table.

"I'm a writer, and this old Smith-Corona has seen about five thousand miles. Can't tell you how many times I've changed the ribbon." Legna then stepped back and stared at the typewriter and the wood table as if seeing them for the first time. "You know my father was a carpenter. He made this table for me. We even had our own furniture store in town … made tables, chairs, anything from wood. Daddy loved to work with his hands, and I love to write. Can you understand that?"

Sammy nodded his head, just as he nodded again when Legna said his room was at the top of the stairs, and it was time to go to sleep.

In the dim light, an oak staircase climbed and rose up to the landing on the second floor. Mounting the stairs, Sammy held onto the polished oak banister, and the stairs squealed and seemed to speak to him from under his feet. Once in his room, Sammy propped the picture of his mother on the dresser. As he stared at his mother's picture, a sadness came over him. Could he ever accept or escape his mother's death?

Sammy then sprawled across a bedspread, with race cars that glowed in the dark, and listened to the moan of the wind pry at his window like stiff fingers. Odd sounds, sounds he never heard before, came from the clapboard house on Red Oak Lane.

As he glanced around his darkened room, a slice of moonlight poured across the dresser and illuminated the picture of his mother resting against the mirror. Staring into the amber pool of light, it made the wood on the dresser appear as a shiny patch of honey and soothing to the eyes. He needed to find a soothing place. His room would be his refuge; and Sammy would adjust to his new home and the town of White Chapel, where horses outnumbered people. But could he adjust to Max, who like Tarzan, called him not by his name, but called him *boy*? And could he adjust to a man, who before going to bed at night, kissed the silver urn with his mother's ashes?

Chapter 3

The gilt-framed portrait of Max's mother, enshrined in the center of the dining room wall, presided over the family like a stubborn ghost. Her hair, the color of molten silver, and dark eyes, spaced further than most, appeared to gaze down at Legna as she arranged the last place setting on the table. The clang of silverware and the smell of pot roast, smothered in onions, filled the space as Max came up beside her.

"Now, why don't ya let the boy set the table," he said. "Let'em earn his keep."

"I don't mind, and this is woman's work." She then edged closer to Max and spoke above a whisper. "You know, today is our first dinner together as a family. I made the roast you like, and since Sammy hasn't had a birthday party in years, I made a red velvet cake for dessert. Thought we could put candles on the cake and sing Happy Birthday."

Max grumbled his reply as Legna busied herself filling the glasses with water. But they both turned when Sammy stood in the doorway.

"Can I help?" he asked.

"Kinda late for that. Everything's done," Max said.

Legna's hand tightened around the handle of the pitcher before placing it back on the table. "Let's all sit down now," she said, "before everything gets cold." Then with heads bowed and hands folded, Legna recited *Grace*. After the prayer, Max leaned back in his chair and glanced up at the portrait of his mother. Staring at his mother's portrait, his face appeared pasty and white as the mashed potatoes that passed from hand to hand.

But when a bowl of asparagus was placed in front of Sammy, his face reddened as he passed it to Max. "I can't eat asparagus," Sammy said. "If I do, I'll break out in hives."

Max clenched his fist and pounded it on the table. "If I didn't eat everything on my plate, I'd get my ears boxed. You take some, boy, I wanta see if ya break out in hives."

"That's all right," Legna said, glaring at Max. "Next time I'll make something else."

No one spoke, and in the silence with the portrait of his mother bearing witness, Max got up from his chair, grabbed the bowl of asparagus and slammed it to the floor. The bowl shattered and the asparagus lay on the wood floor, scattering like thin green pencils. Max then stomped from the room.

Sammy was the first to speak. "Why would Max adopt someone he doesn't even like?"

"But he does like you. It's just sometimes his temper gets the best of him."

Holding back tears, Legna watched as Sammy began gathering shards of glass and stems of asparagus into a pile. "Here, let me do that," she said. "You may cut yourself." After gathering up the debris of vegetables, Legna sat back in her chair and hid the sigh that rose from her chest. She then stared at Sammy and the cake she made, which was to be his birthday cake. Trying to steady her voice, Legna could only say, "Have some dessert. It's a red velvet cake with cream cheese frosting."

Chapter 4

Legna stared at the paper in the typewriter searching for the words to type. And as she sat in the quiet of the knotty pine kitchen, knots in the wood appeared as brown eyes glaring back at her, holding her captive in writer's purgatory where blank minds retreated.

In a kitchen, lost in a prism of time, Legna turned her gaze to sunlight that bathed the room in white. But in the sunlight, chrome on the table and chairs revealed pits of rust and the dried up leather chairs appeared a gaudy crimson red. An oak table and chairs would compliment the knotty pine kitchen, but the chrome set had belonged to Max's mother. Anything left in the house after she died became a permanent fixture, like the clock hanging in the dining room — a black ceramic cat with a tail that wagged back and forth like a dog; and at the stroke of each hour, the cat let out a hideous meow. Below the feline clock sat a white clothes presser from the fifties called a mangle. Since his mother's death, it had never been used and now clay pots with a jungle of ivy spiraled down from the top of the mangle.

But what Legna detested the most was the sitting room couch and chair, the patriotic furniture with a pattern of a bald eagle and American flags flying in the wind. The lumpy, red, white, and blue furniture, encased in plastic, had saggy cushions and couch springs that whined. Yet Legna vowed when Max visited his cousin Charlie in California, the mangle would disappear along with the rusted kitchen set, and the plastic would be peeled from the patriotic furniture.

Legna glanced again at her typewriter. Yet her mind remained frozen like icicles dangling from the gutter outside the window. There were times she felt the loneliness, the solitude that comes with being a writer. But her heart quickened when she thought of her memoir and writing about a boy named Sammy, who changed her life.

As Legna began typing, Max came into the kitchen wearing black rubber boots and his twenty pound deer skin jacket that caused his shoulders to sag. Standing over Legna, he grabbed the pencil by her typewriter and broke it in half. "Ya gonna sit there all day writin' in that old stained robe?" Max then stared at dishes stacked in the sink and plates and glasses scattered across the table. "Now jess looke here at all this mess."

After glancing at the stack of dishes, Legna lowered her head and stared down at her chenille robe with splotches of ink marking the front. Then raising her tall frame from the chair, and dressed in a fuzzy robe that touched the floor, she appeared as a six foot stalk of beige chenille. Moving over to the sink, Legna slipped her hands into the sudsy water and began scouring a cast iron skillet.

Max sat down at the table with his eyes fixed on Legna.

Then in the quiet, Legna began drying forks and spoons and dropping them, piece by piece, into the drawer. She was the first to speak. "What are you doing today?"

Max grumbled, as if trying to gather the words in his throat before he spoke. "The sheriff's coming by. We gotta discuss some things."

"Is he bringing a prisoner's body to be cremated?"

"Don't know, but that's not yur worry. Jess worry about cleaning up this mess."

Legna watched from the window as Max left and disappeared into the cinder block building where the furnace he called the *beast* provided a final resting place for those choosing cremation. Yet as she watched sunlight cast bright rays over the crematory, it still appeared cold and stark. Even in sunlight, darkness prevailed, and the block and mortar of the crematory seemed to hold secrets of the dead buried within.

From dust you came and to dust you shall return,
she recited in her mind. But running a crematory
had become a way of life for Max, a life he grew up
with and inherited from his parents.

The sun beckoned Legna away from the
typewriter, and she slipped her coat over her robe
and pulled on her boots. Walking into the morning
air, she followed a path of melting snow, darkened
by the brown hungry earth struggling to emerge
from its winter slumber. As sunlight warmed Legna's
shoulders, she climbed down the crest of a hill
toward the crematory. When she saw the sheriff's
Jeep parked in front of the building, she thought of
asking Clyde about his wife, Edith, who had been ill
and absent from church for weeks. Venturing inside,
she listened as the sheriff spoke in a rough tone from
Max's office. But what she heard next made her
stand frozen and afraid to breathe.

"Don't matter if we bury them or have them
cremated," the sheriff said. "They're dead anyway.
When the state sends a check to bury them, we save

them money by cremating them. Even though that money goes right in our pockets."

"Just hope none of them prisoners ever have to be exhumed," Max said. "Them ole stuffed shirts on the prison board will be in for a shock when they find empty graves at Restland Cemetery."

"You know, I even plant grass over the grave and around the headstone," the sheriff said. "I make them empty graves look real pretty." And they both burst into laughter.

Moving across the floor, Legna could only hear her breath and the whisper of her coat brushing against the top of her boots. Easing the door shut, she ran back to the house. Once inside, Legna hung her coat over the chair and sat down at her typewriter. But her fingers, which normally danced across the keys, stiffened as she typed the chapter in her memoir about Max. She felt torn, betrayed by the husband she thought she knew.

But Legna was unaware there would be a chapter to come far more terrible than she could imagine.

Chapter 5

Sammy watched Legna raise the lid of a small rosewood chest on her dresser. Taking out the pearl-handled pistol, she held it as if cradling a newborn baby.

"When you hold a gun, always assume it's loaded," she said. "And point the gun away from yourself and anyone around you. This gun isn't loaded, and it's a good pistol to teach you how to shoot. If you tried to shoot the Remington rifle above the fireplace, it would knock you back ten feet."

Sammy, who would rather shoot marbles than bullets, stared at the pistol in Legna's hand.

"Do it for Max," Legna said, seeing the apprehension on Sammy's face. "He thinks everyone should know how to handle a gun. It'll make him happy." Legna paused and gave Sammy a deep stare. "Did you know you came downstairs last night at about 11:30," she said. "You went to the refrigerator, poured milk into a glass, and sat down and ate some cookies. Swear it was like you were asleep. But when you went back to bed, I don't think a hurricane could have raised you."

Sammy hesitated, wondering how to explain that his thinking had changed since the death of his mother. But he only replied, "Sometimes … I don't know if I'm asleep or awake. I don't remember coming downstairs."

"We best start locking the deadbolt. You'll be asleep and walking down Route 22 in your pajamas. And I've been meaning to ask about your first day of school. You haven't said much."

Sammy lowered his head and studied the roses swirled across the rug. Staring down at the floor, he thought about his first day at White Chapel High School. Everyone knew he had been adopted by the family who owned a crematory; and when he went to biology class a small pile of ashes sat in the corner of his desk. A moon-faced boy with pimples dotting his cheeks, like tiny red beads, then poked Sammy from the seat behind him. When the boy spoke, his blemishes scattered on his cheeks. "Those are ashes from your crematory. And I saw you riding through town in your hearse. You looked pathetic and tried to hide. But I saw you."

Once Sammy would have raised his fist to the boy, but he remembered what he learned from Father John. *They're only words. Nothing more.*

"Sammy ... Sammy," Legna repeated. "Well, how was school?"

"Fine. It was fine."

When they walked out into the hallway, Sammy stopped in front of the wedding portrait of Max and Legna hanging in a brown oval frame. A younger Max with a thick head of hair stood smiling, while Legna clutched a bouquet of white roses and appeared stoic. "How long have you and Max been married?"

Legna glanced down at her wedding ring. "About twenty years. Max was my second cousin, and I was close to his mother. After she died, he had no one. Soon a friendship turned to flowers and my favorite chocolates. And on Friday nights, we would go to the Grange Hall and dance the two-step until midnight." Legna paused, and clasped her hands together. "I know Max can be difficult. Wasn't always that way. When he was about your age, he was thrown from a horse. Almost died. The doctor put a silver plate in his head and it changed him. But God put Max in my life for a reason."

"Why's that?" Sammy asked.

"He needs me, and I promised his mother before she died I would take care of him. But right now we need to go out back. Max is waiting for us."

When they walked into the back yard, Max stood lining tin cans on the fence rail. Positioning each can in a row, he stood back and eyed the cans, as if he had an imaginary tape measure in his head.

Max then moved forward, eyed the cans again before sliding two closer together.

Legna went over to Max, handed him the pistol, and took her place on the porch, keeping her eyes on Sammy like a lioness watching over her cub. Max then loaded the gun, assumed an official stance, aimed, and fired. When he missed two of the three cans on the fence, he kicked the can on the ground and began to cuss. "I'm just havin' me a bad day. That's all." Max stopped and stroked his mustache, before turning to Sammy. "Come on, boy ... let's see how yur gonna shoot."

When Max slid the pearl-handled pistol into Sammy's hand, it felt like a wedge of ice, as he gave the command "Aim. Pause. Fire."

Holding his arm steady Sammy fired the pistol, and when the bullet pierced the can, it tore through the air like a bird taking flight. Sammy kept firing the pistol, and each time a can ripped through the air, Legna raised her hands with a gesture that urged him on.

As dusk settled in, it stole the sunlight and cast a lavender haze over the sky. In the half-light Legna stepped from the porch and walked over to Max and Sammy. "That was some mighty good shooting," Legna said, resting her hand on Sammy's shoulder. "Real good shooting."

"Good shooting ... good shooting," Max said. "Stop yur fussing over the boy."

Legna's voice dropped. "It's getting dark and we best go inside."

After Legna disappeared into the house, Max swaggered over to Sammy with his legs spread in a cowboy walk. Then clenching his fist, Max pointed a long square finger at Sammy. "Bang, bang ... I got'cha," he said, throwing his head back with a laugh that cut through the night.

Max then drew closer, and Sammy could feel his breath warm his neck before he spoke. "Jess remember this, boy, a gun's made for one reason and that's to kill. And there's no match for a bullet."

As Sammy watched Max's bulky frame retreat back to the house, he stayed behind and thought about what Max had said. But Sammy only felt threatened by one person, and Max hadn't threatened him.

Not yet.

Chapter 6

The next morning while Sammy ate breakfast, Legna sat in her robe typing. It was a Saturday. A day for chores. A day Sammy dreaded. He had already dusted his dresser and swept his bedroom floor, but a new duty had been added to the list of chores kept on the refrigerator — help Max in the crematory. Pushing his oatmeal aside, Sammy got up from the table, passing a sink-full of abandoned dishes and Legna hammering on the typewriter keys as fast as her fingers would go.

Walking toward the crematory, fifty feet seemed like fifty miles as Sammy tried to make his legs move. When he reached the door, he wrapped a sweaty palm around the knob and ventured inside. He then stood under a naked light bulb that shed light across walls which may have once been white, but now were flesh-colored with crusts of paint that appeared as scabs on a wound. And a foul odor hung in the air — a sour wretched smell that mingled with dust floating through the air. If death had a smell, it hung in the air of the crematory. Sammy held his breath as he knocked on the door to Max's office.

Sitting at his desk, Max tilted back in a soft-padded chair, and the chair squealed under the load. "Ya know, I wish people would die. We could use the business." Throwing his head back, Max laughed until his laughter turned into a coughing fit.

But Sammy stood motionless with his eyes circling the room. And through an open section of the wall, he caught a glimpse of the furnace — the *beast*, as Max called it. The slab of gray cement, now blackened with age, had dials, gauges, and a vault-like door that consumed people. Sammy turned away, but as he surveyed the room, it revealed Max's fetish for neatness. Tools hung evenly spaced from hooks, shelves held bottles in perfect rows, and keys were labeled and dangled from nails above Max's head. Even the cement floor was swept clean, except for some crumbs scattered in the corner. When Sammy bent down to pick them up, Max snapped at him.

"Don't touch that, boy ... that's cheese for the mice. Jess come here and sit down. We gotta talk." Max then began to ramble, recounting the story of his life. "I was sixteen when my father died. Quit school and learned how'ta run this place, with help from my cousin, Charlie. And even now, I get no help from Legna. Thinks she's gonna be a famous writer. Have to tell ya, her mind's gone. She's a bit loony." Max paused to twirl his finger on the side of his head. "But she wasn't like that when I married her. Her family owned a big furniture store. They had money. Now every month she gets a check from her trust fund, but she won't share."

When Max folded his arms across his chest, muscles pressed against his long-sleeved shirt like coils of braided rope. He then leaned forward and rested the weight of his arms on the desk. As Sammy stared at Max's bulging forearms, he often wondered about his arms — arms that were always hidden and concealed, even in the summer, by a long-sleeved shirt. Did Max have his mother's name tattooed down his massive forearm? Or perhaps he had *Mother* tattooed and written inside a heart.

Max gazed to his side, as if wishing he were somewhere else, or Sammy was someone else. Then narrowing his eyes, Max reached under his desk. But instead of pulling out a bottle of Mr. Bud Cola, his large fist gripped a gold-colored flask. Max unscrewed the cap, jerked his head back, and guzzled the brew. Then setting the flask down, he began to laugh, exposing all thirty-two teeth in his mouth that were ivory in color and straight as keys on a piano.

"Let's forgetta 'bout Legna," Max said, slurring his words. "Cause yur the luckiest kid that's ever been adopted. Everythin' I worked for is gonna belong to ya." He paused to grin. "Someday, boy, yur gonna own Swinehauser's Crematory."

Sammy swallowed hard and tried to find his words.

"Well, boy, whata ya think?"

"I … never thought about running a crematory. Always thought I'd go to college."

Max said nothing and took another swig from the flask. Then reaching under his desk, he took out a bottle of antacid and drank from the bottle until his lips began to foam. He then took the back of his sleeve and wiped the fizz from his mouth.

But they both glanced up when a fly that survived the cold nights circled the room with tired wings. Sammy lost track of it until the fly buzzed past his ear. He waved his hands to swat it, but then thought of his friend, Goldy, from St. Joseph's Home who would never harm a fly.

"Darn fly," Max said, reaching for the fly swatter.

"I'll … I'll get him." Picking up a newspaper, Sammy coaxed the fly onto the paper and walked to the front door. When Sammy returned, Max threw his head back and laughed.

"Should be prouda ya'self, boy. Ya saved a fly today." Then leaning back in his chair, Max ran his tongue along his teeth, the way he did after eating a chicken dinner, as if trying to savor the meal one last time. Max then waved his arms and dismissed Sammy, much like he had tried to shoo the fly away that buzzed above his head.

As Sammy walked back to the house, the dust of the crematory and the strong smell of whiskey on Max's breath seemed to stay with him. But most important of all, Max's words stuck with him. Max had adopted him not to give an orphan boy a loving home, but to carry on his work at the crematory. Sammy recalled what Max had said, and the words played over and over again in his mind.

'Someday boy, this will all be yours. You'll own Swinehauser's Crematory.'

Chapter 7

Max grumbled as he stood in front of his closet, trying to decide what shirt to wear. Since the day was overcast, much like the day his mother died, he reached for the gray long-sleeve shirt. As Max's mother had done, Legna *used* to leave his shirt and pants hanging on the closet door, starched, pressed, and ready to wear, but things had changed. Max glanced at the knit vest, between layers of tissue paper on the top shelf of the closet. His mother had made it for him. There were times Max moved the vest to another shelf, but it had to be within plain sight, so he could see it each time he opened the closet door.

Max turned to the picture of his mother sitting on the dresser. She had an angular face, and Max had his mother's nose — not too large, but noble. As he stared at the picture, his mother of Italian descent seemed to gaze back at Max with her dark Sicilian eyes. He then planted a kiss on the picture before placing it back on the dresser.

Staring at his mother's picture, he often wondered why she named him Max. It made him think of a shiny car wax, or laundry detergent meant to clean better than any other brand. But his mother told him he was the largest baby born at White Chapel Hospital. He held the record; he was the maximum, the max. He paused to admire his reflection in the mirror. "Yeah, that's me," he said, as he slapped his jowls with some aftershave.

His thoughts then wandered. His mother died about twenty years ago, and Max married Legna the following spring. She was Max's second cousin, with thick wavy hair that seemed to float down and curtain one side of her face. He glanced at their wedding picture on the bureau and recalled the girl he had grown up with. Max remembered how they scaled the oak tree in the backyard, rode horses along

the trails, and then shared a soda at Phil's Pharmacy.
Now they shared the home Max grew up in.

Legna with her high cheekbones, splash of
freckles, and hair the color of cinnamon, resembled
photos of Amelia Earhart. At first the shy spirited
beauty resisted his advances. Yet Max persisted, and
soon Legna stood beside him to take the sacrament
of marriage. But now, after so many years had
passed, Max wondered how Legna had talked him
into adopting Sammy.

Max lumbered downstairs, slouched, imperfectly
vertical, with his enormous crepe-soled shoes sending
squeals through the quiet house. Once in the
kitchen, he read a note scrawled across some paper
on the table. After reading the note, Max could feel
his face redden. Legna and Sammy had gone to the
movies, but she knew Max hated to be alone, hated
the solitude of his own company. When Legna and
Sammy returned, they would be giggling and
smelling like popcorn from the Regency Theater.

Then Legna would tell Max every detail of the movie as he sat listening with a jittery smile.

Opening the pantry door, Max sighed when he stared at a row of cereal boxes. But cornflakes in a stiff cardboard box seemed bland and unappealing. Legna used to make him breakfast, and Max would stuff himself with flapjacks and homemade sausage from Klein's Butcher Shop. Glancing again at the cereal boxes, he closed the pantry door, walked to the refrigerator, and took out a bottle of Mr. Bud Cola.

As Max guzzled the cold drink, he stared outside at the crematory on the far end of the property. Many thought Max had been miscast in his profession, yet for the man who ran on high octane adrenaline, the crematory was the only place Max felt at home. And his home had always been the town of White Chapel, that once had only a pharmacy, a filling station, and a feed store. Now rows of shops, housed in strip malls, and restaurants dotted the land where farms used to be. He remembered how he and his mother, with a pail in hand, gathered wild berries across the lane, even though it pained a woman her size to trek through the dense brush. Their dog, a beige pug named Biscuit, trailed from behind. Max smiled to himself and tried to stifle his laugh. Why hadn't he tried to persuade Legna into adopting a dog rather than a son?

Max wiped the grin from his face, and peered out at the sky whitened by clouds. He then walked outside, and followed a path of matted-down grass leading to the crematory. But Max shuddered when he glanced at an opening in the sky and the gray pencil-thin cloud that seemed to be pointing down at him. Maybe it was an omen. Today was the 13th , and Max kept track of all odd occurrences, like yesterday when a flock of crows lined the roof of the crematory, perched like black pegs, and blending into the dark shingled roof. Max groaned, wondering what the next catastrophe would be.

When he entered the dank cinder block building, Max gazed at shelves lined with jugs, bottles, and a cement floor etched with cracks that had been there since he was a boy. At the far corner of the crematory was the furnace that Max called the *beast*, which could reduce a human to a bucket of ashes. Yet Max had grown accustomed to the smell of death, and the stench that created a dry burning feeling in the back of his throat.

His thoughts then turned to his father. He had run the crematory until his death and introduced Max to a life of disposing of the dead. But after a grim diagnosis, his father became a resident of Pine Hills Sanitarium, a hospital-like institution which treated those suffering from tuberculosis, or the consumption. His doctor then suggested bed rest, tonics, and sassafras tea for the disease that was destroying his father's lungs. But he never got well. Max remembered how his father was isolated at the sanitarium, and would stand waving from the second floor balcony while his mother stood sobbing.

After his father's death, when friends prepared for college, Max left high school and learned how to operate the crematory. Cousin Charlie drove from

California in a '52 Ford to help him. He resembled Max, but was older with a dense mustache and a tattoo of a ship etched into his hairy jungle of a chest. And Charlie rolled his own cigarettes, buying tins of Bugle tobacco and feeding paper, thin as tissue, into the small rolling machine. Then with the cigarette clenched between his teeth, Charlie struck a match and lit the tip as if performing a ritual.

When his father was alive, they would all huddle together in the crematory and smoke Charlie's stash of hand-rolled cigarettes. Max recalled how his father would puff on the cigarette, purse his lips into an oval, and blow perfect smoke rings. His father would then go to the barn and sit on a stool next to his horse, a mare named Bella. Max chuckled to himself remembering it was the same horse his father rode through the V.F.W. just because someone dared him to.

Yet when his father was alive, he spent most days in the crematory. But when scents from the kitchen of roasted lamb, smothered with garlic, and crusty baked bread reached his open window, he came to supper, sat at the table with his overalls covered in ashes, and it was as though the dead had come to dinner.

Max's face softened, and a smile creased his face when he glanced at the picture of his mother sitting on the desk. She used to make his favorite chicken dinner, fill his glass with Mr. Bud Cola, and slather butter on his roll before setting his plate on the table. With his eyes riveted to the picture, Max imagined his mother's dark Sicilian eyes glaring back at him. Taking the picture from the desk, he held it close to his chest and spoke to her as if she were alive under the glass.

"Mother, you would understand. Little Maxim is unhappy, and things have to change."

Chapter 8

Sammy sat up in bed when he heard shouting from the next bedroom. With only a closet wall separating the two rooms, he crept out of bed and tiptoed into his closet. Kneeling down below a picture of Jesus tacked to the wall, he pressed his ear against the paneled wall.

"What you're doing's illegal," Legna said, in a tone louder than she ever spoke. "That money belongs to the state. And if they find out, you and the sheriff are both going to jail."

Max barked back at her. "Jess keep yur nose out'ta my business."

The words died their own death, and then there was silence. As Sammy huddled in the closet, he wondered if Max would ever harm Legna? And if he tried, how would Sammy protect her? He thought of the pistol in the case on Legna's dresser and remembered what Max had said after target practice. 'A gun's made for one reason, and that's to kill.'

He slipped back into bed, tossing and turning, before drifting into a restless sleep. But Sammy was roused from his sleep when he heard a noise. Sitting up in bed, he became conscious of everything around him — the darkness that swelled the room, the sound of the wood floor squealing under the weight of footsteps, and the sound of his heart beating at a frantic pace. As he sat rigid in his bed, he spied the silhouette of a man descending over his room like a large black cloud. Yet as the figure drew closer, it was not an unknown creature lurking in the night — it was Max. Every hair on Sammy's head didn't stand on end, but vibrated to the drumbeat of his heart. Then without uttering a word, Max reached down and clamped giant hands around his neck, squeezing tighter and tighter. Sammy fought back through a tangle of covers, gasping for air, but he felt his last breath was being squeezed from him.

When Max spoke, the words rumbled out. "Made a big mistake comin' here, boy. A big mistake."

Gathering all his strength, Sammy swung his arms and broke free of his grasp. Then with trembling hands, he stroked his neck and began taking deep breaths. *It was a dream, a nightmare, he thought as his eyes circled the room.* He lay still, afraid to move, and calmed his mind by counting blocks of light on the side of the blinds. But soon his eyes grew heavy, and he fell asleep.

When the shrill blast of the alarm sounded, Sammy rubbed the sleep from his eyes. It was 7:45 A.M. Sliding his feet along the floor, he moved zombie-like into the bathroom. As he stared into the mirror, his face grew pale. Running his fingers along his neck, he stared at the red lines covering his neck from one end to the other. Glaring at the marks in the mirror, his words came slow. "It wasn't a dream. Max tried to kill me," he said, in a voice fading to a whisper. Then bending over the sink, Sammy began splashing cold water onto his throat.

Forcing his feet to move, he made his way down the stairs. But when he stood in the doorway of the kitchen, only Legna sat at the table.

"Where's ... where's Max?" Sammy asked.

"He went into town."

Sammy glanced again at Legna. She was quiet and eating with her head tipped down. Her auburn hair, normally combed for breakfast, was a wild mass of curls, disheveled and scrambled like the eggs on her plate. Pulling out the chair, he sat nibbling at his food and spearing the sausage with his fork.

"Better eat, or you'll miss the bus," she said.

But as he pushed a pile of scrambled eggs from one end of his plate to the other, Sammy could feel Legna's stare.

"Your neck looks red," she said. "Your face is sort of red too. Maybe you're getting sick."

Sammy swallowed hard. "Legna," he said, and then he stopped.

"What is it?"

"Would … would Max ever hurt anybody?"

Legna sipped the tea and raised her eyes slowly above the rim of the cup. "Max has a temper. Used to be the playground bully, and nobody argues with him. Ever. But I know how to calm him down. I call him *Maxim* like his mother used to. Works every time."

Legna's hands shook when she set the teacup down, and it rattled on the saucer. As he watched her retreat to silence, he wondered if she feared Max; and if he tried to harm her, how would Sammy protect her? He wanted to be truthful and tell her what Max had done, but who would believe an orphan from St. Joseph's Home? A boy who may be labeled a troublemaker — a boy who made up stories.

Sammy got up from his chair. "I … have to go upstairs. I forgot something."

"Better hurry. The bus comes in ten minutes."

Sammy climbed the stairs, two steps at a time, and ran into Legna's bedroom. Opening the case on her dresser, he carefully removed the pearl-handled pistol. Holding the gun close to his side, he stood in the doorway, looked left to right, and then darted across the hall. Once in his room, he laid the pistol under the pillow and smoothed back his bedspread.

Legna glanced up when Sammy grabbed his book bag from the kitchen table.

"I may not be here when you come home from school," she said, "but don't worry, Max will be here."

Chapter 9

Seated on the couch, Max wore a black shirt and pants and appeared as a huge lump of coal wedged in the corner. But when Sammy entered the room, Max scratched his thinning scalp and buried his head in the newspaper. Sammy felt his fists tighten at the sight of Max, who engaged in psychological warfare, and he began to loathe him. Hatred was a sin, a seed of evil, yet who wouldn't loathe a man who tried to kill him.

Sammy slipped into the kitchen where Legna stood stirring a pot on the stove. She looked up, set down her wooden spoon, and spoke in a hushed tone. "Why did you take the pistol and put it under your pillow? I saw it when I changed your sheets. You're going to hurt yourself. What if the pistol would accidentally go off?"

Sammy swallowed hard and spoke in an exact measured tone he rarely used. "I'm always careful. Thought I'd be ready if anyone broke in."

"That's not a good idea. In fact, it's dangerous. I put the pistol back in the case."

Sammy was dry-tongued, but said nothing. He needed the pistol — needed it to protect Legna from Max. He would take the pistol from its home in the rosewood chest, put it back under his pillow, and start changing his own bedding. Legna trudged back to the stove. "I made some apple fritters. And you know you have to help Max in the crematory." She paused and peered into Sammy's face. "You still don't look well. I think you may be getting sick."

Sammy *was* ill at the thought of being alone with Max, but he didn't have to pretend being sick after eating Legna's stew and vinegar pie the night before. She had cleaned out the refrigerator, gathering up vegetables that were withered and limp, cheese with patches of green mold, and roast beef left over from dinner a week ago. But he stood without expression when Legna placed the flat of her hand on his forehead.

"You've got a fever. Better go on to bed and just forget about your chores."

"Okay," was all Sammy could think to answer. He then climbed the stairs, still nauseated, but now felt a sense of relief. Collapsing on his bed, he pulled the spread of speeding race cars over him and fell asleep. He woke up when Legna entered his room.

"I brought you up some ginger tea. My mother used to make it when I was sick. First you grate the ginger, boil it, and then strain it. Settles your stomach and will cure whatever ails you." Legna placed the cup of tea on the nightstand, and then sat on the edge of the bed with her hands gripping her stomach. At first the sound from her lips was that of a long-held groan, and then she forced the words out. "You know, I don't feel well either. Must have been that extra piece of vinegar pie I ate."

After Legna left the room, waves of nausea swept over him, and he began to sweat, as if the meal she made was trying to escape, leech its way from his body. Then with half-closed eyes, he watched Legna come back into his room, padding across the floor in her soft-soled slippers. Standing over his bed, she smiled while smoothing down his blanket. As the door closed behind her, Sammy vowed he would help Legna prepare meals — study every cookbook she had. Or die of food poisoning.

Sammy then began massaging the knot in his stomach, trying to forget how the stew looked on his plate — a heap of mustard-colored lumps covered with bits of green. And each time he thought of Legna's stew, the ball in his stomach grew harder. He finally fell asleep, and when he woke up, the glass on his window appeared as if it had been painted black. It was midnight, and as he lay in the dark, there was no stream of chatter from Legna who could be heard speaking in muffled tones. There was only quiet. Soon he drifted back to sleep.

When morning came, sunshine washed over Sammy's face, and he closed his eyes to shield them from the light. Curled in the hollow of his bed, he wiped the band of sweat from his forehead. With his heart pounding, he flung back the mound of blankets that weighed heavy on him. *Perhaps it was his imagination. An illusion or a dream.* But as he began to remember, it left him shaking, and he pulled the blankets back over him.

As he had done before, Max slipped into Sammy's room during the night. His heart quickened when he remembered the slow heavy tread of his boots dragging across the wood floor as Max drew closer and closer. Then standing over him, instead of using his giant hands for weapons, Max raised the barrel of a rifle. 'Shoulda never come here, boy. It's gonna be like it was before ... jess me and Legna.'

Sammy tried to holler, tried to shout Legna's name, yet he could not make a sound. But before Max could fire the rifle, Sammy reached under his pillow and grabbed Legna's pistol. Sweat poured from his face, and it happened in a reckless moment

—in the flash of a second. Sammy pulled the trigger; the shot pierced his chest, and Max slumped to the floor.

No ... No, Sammy howled inside himself. He lay motionless, unable to move, as if he too had been shattered by the blast of the gun. But there was no body, no blood on the floor, and no pistol under his pillow. Had Max crawled under his bed after he was shot, and if he looked there, would he be staring into the eyes of a dead man? He slipped out of bed, and moving like a thief in the night, reached for the baseball sitting on the shelf. Positioning the ball, he rolled it across the floor and under the center of his bed. When the ball rolled out from the bed, and bounced off the baseboard, he began to breathe again. There was no body under the bed, and it had to be a dream. Or was it?

Sammy calmed his mind as he took his Sunday suit from the closet. Scrubbed clean and dressed for church, he slicked back his hair and slid on his new loafers. Then with timid steps, he went into Legna's room and lifted the lid of the chest that housed the pearl-handled pistol. Sammy drew in his breath as he stared inside the *empty* chest. Closing the lid, he tried to steady his legs as he made his way down the stairs. But when he passed the kitchen, his eyes were drawn to the window above the sink. He stared at the rhododendron bush, framing the window, and clusters of flowers that appeared a blur of white. Edging closer, he saw the sheet of plastic pulled tight and taped over the window.

When he went into the sitting room, Legna sat so still, she could have been posing for a picture. She smoothed the wrinkles from her skirt before looking up.

"What happened to the kitchen window," Sammy asked, "the one above the sink?"

"Last night around 1:00, I heard a loud noise. Like a crash. And when I came downstairs, the window was broken. There was glass everywhere."

"Probably those McMillan boys again," Sammy said. "Out breaking windows and causing trouble."

"Surprised you didn't hear the window break," Legna said. "But once you're asleep, a hurricane couldn't raise you."

"I didn't hear anything. And where ... where's Max?" Sammy asked.

When Legna spoke, her eyes filled with tears. "I woke up and Max was gone. So was his suitcase." She hesitated. "I should just tell you. Max and the sheriff were taking money illegally from the state. Pretending to bury inmates at the cemetery. But they saved money by cremating them, and then both pocketed the extra money." Legna stopped and dabbed the corner of her eyes. "Maybe Max thought someone found out, and he had to get out of town. But one thing I don't understand is how he left. He didn't take the car ... it's still here."

"What are we going to do? I can bag groceries at Ferguson's Market after school."

"There's no need to worry about money. Every month I get a check from my trust fund."

Legna lowered her head and buried her fists in her hair. As he watched her collapse into the couch, Sammy knew it was not a dream. But how could he tell Legna he killed Max? Shot him in the chest with her pistol.

With a tear-stained face and auburn hair tousled about her face, Legna glanced up at the clock. "It's 9:00. We best leave for church. Sometimes all we can do is pray."

The tires of the hearse dug into the gravel road as they drove toward Saint Michael's Parish. But Legna was quiet and said nothing when they passed the *House of Pancakes* where they stopped each Sunday after church and devoured stacks of pancakes. Legna always ordered blueberry pancakes, and Sammy had waffles topped with strawberries and whipped cream. They usually sat in a corner booth, and Legna seemed to repeat the same story of how Max used to go to mass until they caught him taking money from the poor box. God and everyone at church would have forgiven him she would say; but Max never came back to church.

Today when they drove by the pancake house, Legna stared straight ahead and clutched the steering wheel until her knuckles turned white. When she found her words, her voice trembled. "Max isn't coming home. He's not coming back," she repeated.

Max *wasn't* coming home and Sammy was a killer. Yet there were things he didn't understand — things which appeared to be a mystery within a mystery. Where was Max's body? And what happened to Legna's pearl-handled pistol?

Chapter 10

A curtain of trees blended with sycamore and pine; and wrapped at their base, vines shot out new growth filled with tender berries. Weeds were dense, the grasses and nettle high. And bordering the clearing, evergreens melted into the sky, scenting the woods with the smell of pine. Yet after combing and searching the woods behind Legna's house, Sammy found no trace of Max, no body or gun. His only discovery was a neat pile of ashes next to a sycamore tree.

Also in a neat pile in the driveway, waiting for the Salvation Army truck to come by, was the mangle, the chrome kitchen set with rusted legs, and the cat clock with the hideous meow. Soon after, an oak table and chairs with blue plaid cushions graced the kitchen. Then with scissors in hand, Legna cut off the plastic that covered and protected the patriotic furniture from even a speck of dust. Legna seemed to know — Max *wasn't* coming home.

With the money from Legna's trust, the *beast* no longer had to consume flesh to provide income for the family. Even though the crematory was silent, Sammy found himself going to the cold dank building and leaving bits of cheese for the mice who had taken refuge there.

Although Max was gone, his shadow, his presence, remained in the house. But life began to appear normal, as if a scar had formed over Sammy's heart, covering up the horrible deed he had done. Yet he waited for the police to come, and knew he wouldn't be able to look at Legna's face when he put his hands behind his back and was led away in cuffs. Sammy wondered where a sixteen year old boy would go to prison, and thought of men in orange jumpsuits, with thick tattooed arms, who lived to prey on young boys.

Sammy waited for a knock on the door, and on a Saturday afternoon, he knew the balding man in a

tweed jacket was a detective. The man, slight of
build, flashed his badge and came inside, walking in
black spade shoes that appeared too tight for his feet.
When he spoke, he had a dull flat tone and a distinct
pattern to his speech. "Mrs. Swinehauser, I'm
Detective DeLuca. You remember, we've met before,
but I didn't catch your son's name."

Legna rested her hand across Sammy's shoulder.
"This is my son, Sammy."

The detective locked eyes with Sammy and gave
him an intense stare. And Sammy wondered if he
was like Father John; could he see inside his soul?
Detective DeLuca then came and stood next to
Legna. "Max has been missing about six months
now. Has anyone heard from him?"

"Nobody has. Even called his cousin, Charlie, in
California, and he hasn't heard from him."

The detective took out a notepad and printed
"Motive" and underlined it twice. "Now who would
want to harm Max? People usually don't just
disappear. And I'm sure you're aware Max and the

sheriff were taking money illegally from the state. Maybe this whole scheme started to make the sheriff nervous. Nervous enough to get rid of Max."

Legna's face grew tight and pale. Her hands shook. Although she knew what Max had done, Legna never thought the sheriff would harm him.

"Has the sheriff ever threatened your husband?" the detective asked.

Legna hesitated before she spoke. "I don't think he ever did."

"You know, the sheriff's a person of interest in your husband's disappearance. People can get greedy. The sheriff may have wanted *all* the money from the state."

The detective then covered his mouth and began to cough, a barking cough that echoed through the room. "Excuse me," he said. "Can I have a glass of water?"

"How about some lemonade?" Legna asked. "I made some this morning."

"No thanks. Water's fine."

When Legna left the room, Detective DeLuca sat erect with his hands clasped together on his briefcase. As his eyes surveyed the room, they came to rest on the rifle above the fireplace. He then turned to Sammy. "Do you know how to shoot a gun?"

Sammy began to stutter. "I … I can only shoot a pistol."

"Oh…. you know how to shoot a pistol?"

"Yes sir."

The detective fixed his eyes on Sammy, but looked up when Legna handed him the glass of water. Taking a long swig, he rattled the ice in a near-empty glass before setting it on the table. Then reaching into his pocket, he slipped a small white card into Legna's hand. "Call me anytime. You know, I don't want to brag, but they say I'm like a bloodhound. I'll search, I'll sniff out the truth … and I'm gonna find out what happened to Max."

Detective DeLuca then turned and walked outside. As he made his way into the back yard, he scaled the crest of a hill, with the tips of his pointed shoes digging into the soft dirt. Walking down a worn path of grass, he stopped when he came to the crematory. Raising his short frame, he peered inside the paned-glass window. Sammy watched from the porch as the detective reached into his briefcase and began scribbling notes on a long white pad.

Then getting into his station wagon, Detective DeLuca drove off with his car sinking into the gravel road and powdering the trees and bushes with dust. But before the detective sped away, he turned and glared back at Sammy. As Sammy watched his car disappear from sight, he wondered why Detective Deluca stared back at him. Did he know the secret Sammy harbored, a secret darker than anyone could imagine? He could almost hear the detective say in front of a packed courtroom:

"Ladies and Gentlemen of the jury, Sammy is responsible for Max's death."

Chapter 11

Weeks turned to months, and Detective DeLuca never returned to question Legna about Max, the man who shared her life and called her *Mother*. And he never came with handcuffs to haul Sammy off to live with men in orange jumpsuits and thick tattooed arms. Detective DeLuca vanished from their lives like Max had vanished.

As summer ended, trees shed their leaves, and an open field appeared dusty and barren when the county fair hitched up its trailers and left town. Prize-winning cows were herded home, children whined for one more ride on the carousel, and housewives boasted of winning a blue ribbon for their apple pie. Only remnants of the fair remained. With popcorn boxes from the fair littering country roads, maple trees blazed with color awaiting the arrival of fall and senior year to begin at White Chapel High School.

When senior year arrived, the shadow of a beard covered Sammy's face; he grew broad-shouldered and tall. And gripping the steering wheel of the hearse, and with Legna seated beside him, he learned to drive. But when he stepped on the gas pedal, the hearse bucked like a wild stallion as Legna held onto the dashboard. 'Go slow on the gas. Ease up on the clutch,' Legna could be heard repeating. But with practice and in time, Sammy had a car of his own and no longer drove a car seen only in funeral processions.

When he drove his Chevy on the roads of White Chapel, it would prove to be a distraction, an escape, just as Sammy learning to cook would become a distraction. And after studying Legna's collection of cookbooks, he won his way into her heart by searing, dicing, broiling, and whipping up soufflés that puffed to a delicate golden brown.

Now the sound of chicken filets, being pounded a quarter inch thick, could be heard along with Legna pounding the keys of her typewriter.

"Someday you're going to be a great chef," Legna would say. "Maybe even have your own restaurant. I'm going to write that in my book." With a far off look in her eyes, Legna sat as an open vessel, in an alpha state, writing about the adopted son who changed her life. She sat not in her chenille robe, but dressed in a denim shirt and slacks with her hair pulled back from her face and her lips painted a soft shade of red.

But Legna had become a self-made widow, viewed with suspicion over the disappearance of her husband. Yet when she ventured into town, she carried her head high, passing women who raised thin-veined hands to cover their whispers when she walked by. Unfazed and with straight shoulders, Legna would go into Sabol's Flower Shop and buy a cluster of daisies. Returning home, she hummed to herself as she arranged the flowers in a vase that sat next to a picture of Max — the husband who had become a memory.

When Sammy boarded the door of the crematory, Legna stood beside him and held the hammer and nails. The *beast,* now silent, no longer spewed out smoke or the smell of death. Even the mice, who made the crematory their home, moved on. Everyone moved on but Sammy. It was as if a hand, other than his own, had fired the shot that killed Max. Sammy's guilt would become a prison without bars, and his conscience would gnaw away at him like termites devouring a piece of wood. And on a storm-filled night, after a clap of thunder rattled his room, he imagined the figure of Max standing over his bed.

But Sammy never meant to harm Max. Staring down the barrel of his rifle, he had no choice but to fire the shot that killed Max. Getting up from his bed, he stood in the exact spot in his room where Max had taken his last breath. In his mind, he imagined the blast of a gun. Sammy jerked, shuttered, and staggered back to bed, feeling a deep piercing pain in his chest. As he lay in bed, wondering if he would ever sleep again, his thoughts turned to the most devout man he knew. Sammy would go and see Father John from St. Joseph's Home. Hidden by the screen of the confessional, Sammy would confess what he had done and Father John would ask God to forgive him.

But Sammy wondered if he would ever be forgiven.

When Sammy arrived at St. Joseph's Church, he parked in the lot adjacent to the church. Clutching the steering wheel, he gazed at the front of the church, guarded by a stone angel with outstretched arms and wings covered in a cloak of moss.

When he entered the church, stained glass windows blazed with sunlight and cast a rainbow across the large gold crucifix above the altar. With the crucifix showered in sunlight, Sammy blessed himself and took a seat in the back pew. Beside him, clutching rosary beads, a woman held onto church traditions with her tight gray curls draped with a linen handkerchief. Then with hands folded together, she raised her head and rolled her eyes toward the ceiling as if it were the sky. The woman then began to mutter with no words coming from her lips.

As the saintly woman prayed, and with a stream of parishioners filing in and out of the confessional, soon it was Sammy's turn. All eyes were upon him, or was this his imagination? Timid steps led him into the confessional, and he sat down on the cold wooden seat.

Father John slid open the grilled window and began to pray in his distinct Irish Brogue. He then listened as Sammy recited, "Bless me, Father, for I have sinned. It's been two months since my last confession."

"What are your sins?" Father John waited, but there was no response. "My son, what are your sins?" he repeated.

"I missed mass on Sunday," he said, in a voice unlike his own. "I lost my temper. I … I did something I'm so ashamed of. But … it was an accident."

"To absolve you of your sins, tell me what you've done."

A lump rose in Sammy's throat, and he was unable to confess the sin that weighed on his heart. As he kneeled in the confessional, the silence was deafening. He was relieved when Father John spoke.

"Never forget that Jesus loves you … He died for you." Father John paused. "I can tell you're troubled. That you have a burden. Did you know when the load of an animal is too great, they will sink to their knees? Refuse to move. You must do the same. Fall to your knees and ask Jesus to help you."

For a moment, a feeling of peace settled over him. Sammy made the sign of the cross and left the confessional; but he turned when a loud voice boomed in his head — *Thou shalt not kill!* He jerked his head around, yet the only movement in the empty church was sunlight streaming through the stained glass windows. He then kneeled down in the pew, bowed his head, and began to recite *The Lord's Prayer.* But as he sat back in the pew, feelings of shame and guilt consumed him. Would he carry his secret to the grave?

And would his secret stay buried forever?

Chapter 12

When Legna answered the door, Sally Fletcher, from the property down the road, stood on the porch. A slight woman under five feet tall, Sally wore Mary Jane shoes, navy slacks, and with the collar of her blouse meeting her chin, she was dressed more than modesty required. Her hair, once the color of a copper penny, was tamed into a bun and rested atop her head like a smooth gray stone.

Sally came inside and sat next to Legna on the couch. She then took a deep sigh and said *God Bless* as she did each time before she spoke. "I was just thinking about you. Poor dear. How long now has Max been missing?"

"It's been almost three years," Legna said.

"Hard to believe a person can vanish like that. Just disappear. Never heard of such a thing. And

how are you managing with Sammy away at school?
Must be awfully lonely being here all by yourself."

"I'm doing fine. Sammy comes by on weekends.
And someday he's going to be a great chef."

Sally's lips formed a polite smile. She then
sighed, wrung her hands together and rested them on
her lap. "You know, dear, there's something I've
always wanted to tell you," she said. "Before Max
went missing, I saw smoke coming out of the
crematory. Must have been around midnight. You
know I don't sleep well. Never saw smoke coming
from the chimney at that hour before."

"I don't know why," Legna said. "But Max was
doing a lot of things I didn't understand."

"I know. And I'm sorry I haven't come by lately,
but I've been so busy. I was nominated President of
our African Violet Society. But we should try to get
together, like we did when my dear Chester was
alive. We had such fun. You always brought the
apple cobbler … apples were always a bit too hard,
but oh well, no one's perfect." Sally paused and

glanced out the window. She then tensed her round, cherub-like face that was still supple and firm. "You know, I better run along. Looks like a storm's brewing."

Sally left and Legna sat in a room where light no longer filtered through the lace curtains. As dark clouds gathered, she sat thinking, listening to the sounds of the wood frame house. The kitchen window rattled, alerting her of the coming storm, and a loose shutter sounded like a door slamming each time it banged against the house.

When Legna switched on the lamp, tiny yellow flowers painted on the glass shade swirled around the room like fireflies on a summer night. Her eyes then came to rest on the brown grainy picture on the wall. Legna was about six years old, a child in Sweden, as she waded through a sea of wildflowers. Her burning bush of curls was tied back with a ribbon, and her mother had stitched the dress she wore, a pale-colored pinafore that seemed the same shade as the sky.

Legna's thoughts drifted back to that spring day. Her father had been in the barn sanding a round wooden table. She remembered sitting in the hay watching his hands move across the rough oak boards, and he seemed to become one with the wood. After he brushed piles of sawdust aside, a table top slick as marble appeared. She remembers stroking the wood with her fingers, the sweet smell of the oak, and how her father's brown hair was sprinkled with sawdust. A warm feeling came over Legna when she recalled her father's face as he stared at the table, and how his lips raised to a smile.

Leaning back in her chair, Legna glanced at the picture of Max, sitting next to a vase of flowers. She remembered Max coming to the door with roses in one hand and an imaginary lasso in the other that he intended to use to rope her into marrying him. Yet after taking their wedding vows, Legna vowed to mold Max into the man she wanted him to be. But something happened. The world had done things to Max, changed him, but he had done far more to himself. He even threatened to send Sammy back to St. Joseph's Home.

But when she thought of Sammy, a smile crossed her face. He was now a tall broad-shouldered man, and for $95.00 a month rented an apartment in town not far from the culinary school he attended. His tree-lined street housed an Italian café, a barbershop, and rows of brownstone buildings. His apartment stood above Barton's Bakery, the oldest bakery in town, and the smell of fresh baked bread often filled his small apartment.

Legna walked into the kitchen, took a sweet roll from the box and set it on the plate. Lifting the lid of the kettle, she poured water into the teapot and waited for the familiar whistle from the green-enameled pot. She then sat down at her typewriter.

Once straight and erect, her frame now appeared curved and bent; and each winter the arthritis deepened in her knees. She often wondered who the woman was staring back at her in the mirror with eyes faded as a pair of denim jeans and a face creased like parchment paper. But when Legna sat down at her typewriter and began to write, she was young again. Smoothing back strands of hair, once a flame of red, her fingers danced across the keyboard at a steady rhythm.

Legna would finish her memoir, with each chapter a story of her life. She would write about the boy from St. Joseph's Home who changed her life.

Chapter 13

Sammy parked in the bed of gravel next to Legna's house, bordered by a screen of hedges. Within weeks, the hedges had grown uneven, misshapen, with straggly branches jutting out from the privet hedge. Sammy retrieved the clippers from the shed, and as he began snipping the branches, he heard footsteps behind him.

"So glad the gardener's returned," Legna said, as she edged closer. "Swear those hedges grow a foot a day."

Setting down the clippers, Sammy hugged Legna, the woman who rescued him after his mother died — the woman who came to own a piece of his heart.

Linking arms, they walked onto the porch. Once inside the house, Sammy took in all the sights of everything that had once been his home. Curtains filtered the morning sun, daisies in a glass vase brightened the walnut table, and Legna's memoir, next to her typewriter, had grown inches higher.

Legna sat down at the table, sweetened her tea, and took sips from a blue mug, with her brows raised and eyes fixed on Sammy. He came and sat down beside her.

"I've been meaning to tell you, I read in the paper about some burglaries," Sammy said. "One was not too far from your house. On Charles Street. Make sure to keep your doors locked, especially the deadbolt."

"I remember when you could keep your door unlatched. But no more."

As he watched Legna sip her tea, Sammy wondered if he should ask her something he thought about for some time. He searched for the words before he spoke. "But you shouldn't worry, you have your pistol. Someone may think twice about breaking into your house."

Legna was quiet, and gazed down at the table before she spoke. "I don't have the pistol anymore. Just have the Remington rifle. I sold the pistol at Saul's Gun Shop, and put the money toward your schooling."

Legna's hand trembled when she set the mug down on the table, and as their eyes met, Sammy wondered if she knew. *Could she know?* Her pistol was under his pillow when he grabbed it and shot Max, but the next morning the pistol had disappeared along with Max. Was she trying to protect him? Shield him from what happened?

Legna reached across the table and took hold of Sammy's hand. Now, you're not to worry about me. Daddy taught me how to shoot a gun, and I can take care of myself."

As darkness fell, a storm arrived pelting the fields with a cold spitting rain that swept the trees clean. After the rain ended, a dense fog hung over Red Oak Lane, turning the gravel road a deep chalky-gray and covering the fields with a mat of dew.

Through the mist, Sammy drove away as Legna stood on the darkened porch waving with her lips forming the words *goodbye*. Leaving cornfields behind, he drove toward his apartment in town. When Sammy reached the brownstone building, smells from the steel mill mingled with the scent of fresh baked bread from Barton's Bakery. The neon sign above the bakery flashed overhead as he climbed the stairs on the side of the building. Once inside his apartment, he moved through a room consumed in darkness. As a boy he felt threatened by the night, threatened by what might lurk in the shadows.

When Sammy lit the wick of a candle, its flame revealed a room with a brown plaid couch, a matching chair, and two low tables littered with magazines. He then sank into a chair and listened to the familiar chorus of dogs that began each night around 11:00. The dogs seemed to be startled by someone walking home from the night shift at work or someone stumbling home after a visit to the local pub. Sammy had seen one of the dogs, a hound, secured by a heavy chain and tied behind an apartment building a few blocks away. It had brown matted fur and snarled at anyone passing by. But tonight it seemed to be the hound, with a loud gruff bark, that began the marathon of barking. Then a dog with a high shrill bark joined in as if they were arguing with each other. The hound was the last one heard; and as the flame of the candle died out, the barking faded into the night.

Sammy went into the kitchen and put on a pot of coffee. It kept him awake, free from nightmares that once again began to emerge in his dreams. He thought back and remembered, as a boy, riding the carousel with his mother holding him tight on a shiny white horse. As the carousel chimed and spun around, each up and down motion did not bring a smile, but seemed to bring the black panther next to his horse, closer and closer. It had sharp jagged teeth, blood drooling from its mouth, and large plastered claws that dug deep into the carousel floor. For years he screamed in terror at the sight of a black panther. Now the panther seemed to reappear in his dreams, a sign of childhood terror and black as night, with eyes shining green and teeth that could rip into human flesh. In his dream, the panther chased him with the speed of a gazelle, almost getting him within its grasp. Sammy would then waken with his forehead gleaming in sweat and know the panther was his conscience, igniting his own fear and guilt.

The black panther was Max.

Chapter 14

When the alarm sounded at 7:00 A.M., Sammy put his nightmares behind him and the morning ritual began. It was his last day of culinary school, and he had received a message to see his instructor, Chef Paul. Before leaving for school, he filled his thermos with coffee, and put an orange and a ham sandwich into a brown paper sack. Locking the door behind him, he smiled to himself thinking if anyone broke into his apartment, the most expensive item they would find would be the steak defrosting in the refrigerator.

Sammy walked into the silent streets of morning, stepping over a manhole cover spewing mist that rose and blended into the cool damp air. When he passed Barton's Bakery, on the ground floor of his building, he went inside. The bell over the door announced his arrival, and it sounded shrill in the quiet of morning.

A man who stood a few feet higher than the glass counter, wearing an apron smeared with icing, busied himself by lining the shelves with rows of pies. A young girl worked with him, and her face was plain, except for pouty-lips painted with glossy pink lipstick. She adjusted a hairnet over loose brown curls when Sammy walked toward her.

After Sammy bought a cheese Danish, the young girl handed him the pastry in a bag as smooth and white as her porcelain hands. But she seemed to linger when handing him his change. With her palms warm and moist, she slipped the quarter into his hand and then continued filling the case with pastries.

Sammy left the bakery with the bell over the door announcing his departure. He then drove toward Fifth Avenue and *The School for Culinary Arts*. When he arrived at the culinary school, he hurried down the hall and knocked on Chef Paul's door. A portly man answered, dressed in white from his cap down to his soft soled shoes.

"Come in," Chef Paul said, motioning Sammy inside. Chef Paul then rested his large frame behind his desk, pushing aside a half-eaten donut. Taking a seat, Sammy glanced at the awards lining the walls. Chef Paul, a man who traveled the world, had studied in France. He could prepare a four-course dinner, set the table with the proper utensils, and then fold a cloth napkin into an intricate flower design, all in record time. He would then boast. 'You too will become a great chef after graduating from my class.'

Chef Paul leaned back in his chair and folded bulky arms across his chest before he spoke. "Since this is your last day, what are your plans after you graduate?"

"I'd like to find a job in town. I want to stay in Pittsburgh, and be close to the woman who adopted me."

"The Plaza Hotel always asks for recommendations from our graduating class. When Zach, the Manager of The Plaza called, I mentioned your name. He's looking to hire a chef. Why don't you call him and he'll set up an interview?"

Chef Paul reached for a piece of paper and jotted down a telephone number. "Here's his number, and remember to tell him I recommended you."

"The Plaza Hotel … that's the biggest hotel in town. I don't know how to thank you."

But as Sammy held his gaze, Chef Paul squinted his eyes, and they got lost in the plumpness of his face. "There's just one thing," Chef Paul said. "Yesterday someone came by. He flashed a badge and said his name was DeLuca. And I'll never forget his shoes. They were black spades. Haven't seen them in years. Anyway, he was asking how long you've been going to school here. What's the deal? Did you write a bad check, or are you having some money problems?"

"No, it's nothing like that. I don't have any money problems. Everything's fine." Sammy hesitated, took out a handkerchief and mopped the sweat from his brow before finding his words. "The Plaza Hotel would be a great place to work. I want to thank you again for recommending me."

"You don't need to thank me, just remember everything I taught you. And, Sammy, one more thing. Once you start working, pay your rent on time."

Chapter 15

Seated behind a mahogany desk, Zach, the Manager of The Plaza Hotel, flipped through the pages of Sammy's resume. As he studied his resume, Sammy studied the face of an ordinary-looking man, but his face was unreadable. Zach then raised a dark crop of hair and lit the tip of a cigarette. The cigarette smoldered between his fingers, sending smoke climbing over his desk and fading into the gray-colored walls.

Zach then loosened his tie and smiled before he spoke, exposing a gold tooth that shined like a jewel between his lips. "Chef Paul recommended you, and we'll give you a chance. You're hired. Just try not to burn too many steaks. The man who owns The Plaza doesn't like waste. Grew up in the depression. You know what I mean."

When Zach rose from his desk, he was a man small in stature and slim as a boy.

"You can come in on Monday," Zach said. "Around 9:00, and we'll fit you for your uniforms. Right now, follow me. There's someone I want you to meet."

When they walked down the marble hallway, Zach marched with military precision, swinging his arms from side to side. But he stopped when he came to a frosted-glass door that read *Banquet Manager*. Zach then reached into his pocket, pulled out a comb, and smoothed back his hair before knocking on the door.

"Come in," a soft voice answered from behind the glass.

When they walked inside a young woman, dressed in a tan suit, rose from her desk. Her hair, blonde and abundant, tumbled to her shoulders; and she had eyes a shocking blue, almost turquoise in color.

When Zach spoke, he seemed to grope for words. "Beth, I'd like you to meet Sammy Swinehauser. He'll be starting on Monday."

"Nice to meet you," she said, and when she extended her hand, a sweet scent filled the stale office air. An awkward silence followed until Zach stuffed his hands into his pockets, sounding the nervous jingle of coins. Then his square jaw softened. "Beth will show you around, and you'll see why we're the best hotel in town." Pulling up his sleeve, Zach looked down at his watch before heading to the door.

Then like two soldiers who had completed their mission, they marched back down the hall. Zach said little, but when he spoke, he talked to Sammy as if they were old army buddies. "Beth used to be a family counselor before she got into the hotel business. Now she volunteers at some shelter and goes to all those pro-life rallies. But unless you want to carry a sign at a rally, don't get any ideas. She wants nothing to do with men. Believe me, I've tried."

He then watched as Zach's eyes traveled up from Sammy's shoes and to his broad shoulders. His eyes stopped at Sammy's face. "But I wouldn't worry about women. A guy who looks like you should have them beating down his door. Yeah, if I looked like you, I couldn't keep the women away."

After leaving the hotel, Sammy drove to Legna's house in White Chapel. For an instant as he passed fruit trees, with apples begging to be picked, and hills that lay like pillows of moss, he forgot the darkness he harbored; the secret he hid from the world. Free of the city and beneath a cloudless sky, Sammy drove by freshly plowed fields that checkered the landscape with the smell of fresh manure hanging in the air. Further down the lane, he passed Butler's Creek, and it appeared as an open can of green paint, still and untouched by a breeze that stroked the trees.

When Sammy arrived at Legna's house, the peephole on the door glared back at him like a shiny glass eye. As the peephole stood watch, he retrieved his key, unlocked the door and went inside. Sammy called Legna's name, but the only sound was the ticking of the grandfather clock. He then walked out into the yard where a tractor sat, dead and wheel-less, and passed the rabbit hutch, now inhabited by a flock of crows. As he stood in the dry scrub of grass, it seemed August was an unforgiving month. A cluster of petunias clamored for water, and it seemed the only survivors of the summer heat were vines, firm and green, that spiraled from the base of a tree. But when he followed a path leading to the woods, everything appeared lush and green. Under a canopy of trees, a lazy wind stirred leaves overhead and cooled sweat gathered on his brow. And in the quiet, there seemed to be a melody playing for only the trees to hear. Mighty oaks made a ceiling of green, and the shade from their leaves appeared as God's shadow over the earth. Was the visible guided by the invisible with the hand of God touching all creation?

The stillness was broken when a doe and three fawn made their way through the clearing. Their hoofs hit the ground like quiet thunder, and sunlight filtering through the trees caught their sleek brown coats. As generations of deer before them had done, the doe led them to the other side of the clearing. But when they saw Sammy, the two-legged creature who had invaded their home, they jerked around and bolted.

With the air dense with the smell of pine, Sammy moved beyond the clearing. But he stopped when he came to a scant patch of gray next to a sycamore tree. It appeared to be traces of the ashes he found when searching the woods after Max disappeared. Now the ashes were barely visible, beaten down by rain and trampled on by animals. And at the base of the tree, a cluster of marigolds stood all dried and withered.

Sitting down on a mound of rock, Sammy gazed at the ashes. Then taking a stick, he scraped the flattened gray patch and wondered what drove him back to this tree and to the ashes he found after Max disappeared?

Surrounded by quiet, Sammy watched the sun retreat behind a string of trees. As dusk colored the sky with bursts of orange and blue, his heart quickened when he saw the figure of a man scaling the hill below. Against the shadow of dusk, Sammy watched the tall, wiry man. Edging closer, dark hair tangled down to his neck, a plaid shirt covered a wide chest, and chew tobacco dribbled from his mouth. As the man climbed the hill, Sammy felt sweat trickle down his spine when he spied the rifle the man was trying to conceal.

Sammy backed away and ran down a path carved through the brush. But as he stumbled down the hill, he could hear the man hollering. "Hey, I jess wanta ask ya. Wanta go shoot some squirrels?"

Plowing through a maze of wild grass and nettle, Sammy could hear footsteps behind him and dry timber snapping beneath the man's boots. Then like an animal planning his escape, Sammy lunged over a gully filled with rocks and dried briar.

When he found his way past a row of trees, his house appeared in the distance. For a moment he felt safe, but it was an illusion conjured up in his mind. Holding the ache in his side, Sammy's eyes traveled back to the woods, searching for the man with a tangle of hair and chew tobacco dribbling from his mouth. With no one in sight, he squared his shoulders and walked toward the white-framed house. Once inside, he went into the sitting room. On the couch, Legna lay asleep, open-mouthed, with her stocking feet sprawled in front of her and resting next to a sturdy pair of brown-laced shoes. Sitting down beside her, Sammy listened to her shallow breath and the grandfather clock chime and swing its brass pendulum from behind a wall of glass. Legna barely stirred, but when she opened her eyes, they grew wide.

"What happened? You're all covered with sweat."

"I went into the woods. Thought you might be walking the trails. And I saw the strangest man … not far from our house. Wears old clothes, has long hair and carries a rifle."

"You must've seen Otis. Surprised you saw him. He usually roams the woods at night. Lives by himself in the gray-shingled house at the end of the road." Legna paused. "You know, Otis calls me Miss Legna. He's a little slow, but harmless."

"You sure about that?"

"Otis wouldn't hurt anybody. After his mother died, he didn't know what to do. People would find him in the woods, sleeping under a tree. They would tell him to go on home, but he never listened."

"Think he had anything to do with the break-ins we had?" Sammy asked. "Could be someone in the neighborhood."

"I don't think Otis would ever steal from anybody. Believe me, he wouldn't." Legna stopped and combed her fingers through her hair. "I must have fallen asleep. I just came from Sally Fletcher's house … you know, she lives down the street. Anyway, with you being away at school, I gave her a key to the house. Just in case I need her help." She then slid closer to Sammy. "I was so excited when you called. You said you had good news. Well, what is it?"

"I'm going to be a chef at The Plaza Hotel. I start on Monday."

"Oh my, The Plaza Hotel. Do you know how hard it is to get a job there?" Legna rested her arm across Sammy's shoulder. "You've worked so hard and grown into such a fine young man. But then … I always knew you would."

No one spoke, yet there was so much to talk about, so much to be said. In the quiet, Legna took her hand from Sammy's shoulder and placed it over

his hand. And when their eyes met, Legna knew
Sammy had been trying to please her his whole life.

Somehow she knew.

Chapter 16

On his first day at The Plaza Hotel, Sammy walked through the lobby and was drawn to the *Teapot Café*. Gazing above the door of the café, a shiny yellow teapot brewed tea with steam spewing from its long curved spout. When he walked inside, the café held the scent of cigarette smoke and the smell of bacon sizzling on the grill. Taking a seat at the counter, Sammy ordered a cup of black coffee. As he sipped the coffee, a bearish man entered the café, cradling a jacket in his arms as if it were a living thing. He then draped it on the back of the stool beside Sammy. The man then planted himself next to him and spread out hands, like two large paws, almost knocking over the coffee Sammy had set down.

"Morning," the man said, in a gravel voice.

When Sammy turned, his eyes betrayed him. *It wasn't possible.* He stared at the man, inclined to pudginess and bushy silver brows that hung low to his eyes. A fringe of sparse hair circled his head, from ear to ear, contrasting with a dense beard that appeared to be cast from silver. Sammy then glanced down at the man's shirt, unbuttoned and left open to reveal a tattoo on his chest. It was of a ship, with sails barely visible and buried beneath a sea of fuzzy gray hair that covered his upper body. Sammy swallowed hard and tried to find his words.

"Good morning. Sorry for staring, but you look like someone I once knew."

The man's face tightened to a grin. "And I know just who you mean. People told us that all the time, Sammy."

"How … do you know my name?"

"I'm Max's cousin, Charlie, from California, and I know all about you. Even know you're allergic to asparagus. Yeah, Legna sent me so many pictures of you growing up. She told me today was your first day of work, and somehow I knew you'd stop for coffee."

Sammy could only stare at the man who knew far more about him than he liked, a man who resembled an *old Max,* with the tattoo of a ship on his chest and loose-fitting dentures that clicked with each word he spoke. But what intrigued Sammy the most was one of Charlie's eyes ... an eye that seemed to float from left to right, then right to left when he spoke. The traveling eye mesmerized Sammy, and was as strange as the tattoo of a ship buried beneath a cloud of gray hair on his chest.

Charlie then leaned forward and rested his arms on the counter. "Wanna know something," he said. "I came all this way to find Max. Seems no one cares he's missing. Not Legna, not even the police. But I know Max, he would've called me by now."

"I don't know what happened to Max," Sammy said.

"Now hold on," Charlie said. "Just what are you trying to say? You didn't say I don't know where

Max is. You said, I don't know what happened to him. Like he met some awful fate."

Charlie edged closer, narrowed his eyes and spoke in a sullen tone that sounded like Max, a tone that always terrified Sammy. "Maybe Max ended up like toast in the crematory. You know, you could commit the perfect crime. Get rid of a body, and who would ever know? But I'm gonna find Max … and just remember this. I'm like a rattlesnake. If you step on my tail, I'm gonna bite you."

"I hope you find Max. But I have to get to work."

Sammy got up from the stool and left as if fleeing the scene of a crime. Once outside the café, he felt Max had returned from the dead, came back to haunt him. But he would keep the encounter to himself, wouldn't worry Legna about the odd meeting with cousin Charlie. Yet, there were things that were still a mystery, questions which may never be answered about Max's disappearance.

Glancing at the clock in the lobby, Sammy rushed down the hall toward Beth's office. She planned to show him around the hotel, yet he felt spooked. Sammy tried to shake off the bizarre encounter, tried to forget Charlie's accusations.

But could he?

Chapter 17

Sitting in Beth's office, Sammy tried to focus on the wallpaper with a slanted geometric pattern, and the painting on the wall of waves crashing to shore. But he found his eyes fixed on Beth. She wore a black knit dress, heels with a thin ankle strap, and her mane of blonde hair was stacked into a bun, making her appear a few inches taller. He then watched as she fingered some files with long painted nails, and pulled out a folder.

"This will explain our banquet procedures," she said, handing Sammy the manila folder. "And we should meet every Wednesday around 3:00. to go over menus for the following week."

"That's fine. I look forward to working with you." For a moment, their eyes met, but Beth turned away when the phone rang. Seated at her desk, she had a half smile when she spoke. "You know I can't make it. I'm busy. Why don't you ask Mary Ellen?" Beth twirled a lock of hair that fell across her forehead. "I have to go, there's someone in my office." She hung up the phone, and with a sweet scent of flowers trailing behind, walked to the door.

"Let's go down to the kitchen. I'd like you to meet some of the chefs."

As Beth and Sammy walked down the hallway, they were met with stares from the hotel staff. When a busboy, wheeling a cart of dirty dishes, gave Sammy a deep stare he wondered if he knew the secret he hid from the world. Could anyone detect the guilt in his voice or see the shame in his eyes? He pushed the thought from his mind when a woman rushed up to Beth and took her by the arm.

"They took Gladys to the hospital again with those palpitations," she said. "Don't know what we're going to do about the centerpieces for tonight. They're half done and the Harris Group is coming at 7:00."

Beth glanced at her watch. "I can finish them. I'll try to have them done by 5:00."

After the woman hurried off, Beth and Sammy turned down a corridor that led to the kitchen. When she pushed open the kitchen doors, broth simmering in large pots filled the space with scents hard to describe. And in the center of the kitchen, chefs clad in white, gathered around a long griddle as if it were an altar. But amid the chefs in white, and indescribable scents that filled the kitchen, there was a rhythm to the pots and pans clanging in the background. With cleaver in hand, a large-fisted man diced celery and onions with exact precision. And above the sizzle of a frying steak, Beth called out to a man at the far end of the kitchen. "Hey Joel, have you got things handled for the Harris Group?"

A tall slender man swaggered over wearing blue jeans, a western shirt and boots. Glaring at Beth from behind thick dark-framed glasses, he edged closer.

"Everything's on schedule," he said. "Salads are tossed, fruits been cut, and the steaks are ready to broil."

Beth nodded her head. "Joel, I want you to meet Sammy. He'll be working in the main dining room and helping out in banquets."

Joel gave Sammy a half-glance as he turned to Beth. He then took her hand and pulled her aside. Standing over Beth, Joel leaned his arm against the wall, hovering over her like a predator who captured its prey. And Joel stood too close, spoke too loud in a tone that included anyone who cared to listen. Yet Sammy couldn't explain the heat crawling from his neck to his face when he caught bits of their conversation.

"Zach said to let me know if you need anything," Joel said. "Just let me know." He hesitated. "I'll do anything for you."

Beth slipped from under Joel's arm and motioned with her eyes for Sammy to follow. When they left the kitchen, Beth's steps were quick as they escaped down the hallway.

"I have to warn you about Joel. He's Zach's nephew, and if you want to keep your job, be nice to him and…" Beth stopped mid-sentence. "I don't understand why men and women can't be friends. No romantic involvement … just be friends." Beth then walked ahead, rounding a corner and stopping in front of a storeroom with a spacious glass window.

"This is where you'll get your uniforms," Beth said, pointing to rows of white starched uniforms hanging behind the wall of glass. She turned to walk away, but then glanced back. "The Plaza's a great place to work. I think you're going to like it here."

Sammy carried five pair of white pants and five jackets from the fitting room. But before leaving the hotel, he walked by the Gold Room, the largest banquet hall in The Plaza. The door was slightly ajar, and when he peered inside, chandeliers blazed overhead, casting shadows across the sculpted blue carpet. As he glanced around the room, he noticed Beth seated at a table, almost hidden by a wall of flowers and greens.

Sammy knocked on the door and walked inside. "How you making out with the centerpieces?"

"Two more to go, and I'll be done," Beth said.

Sammy laid his uniforms, encased in plastic, over the back of a chair. He then took a seat beside Beth and watched her slide a planter in front of her. After positioning ferns, and red and white carnations into the pot, the bouquet soon looked like a centerpiece in the window of The Fifth Avenue Florists.

"Bet you once worked at a flower shop," he said.

"How did you know? I worked at a florist not far from my college. Went to the University of South Carolina, or the university of spoiled children, as we were sometimes referred to. I have a degree in social services and worked in that field a few years."

"Why did you leave?" Sammy asked.

"I thought I should be doing something else. That I needed a change. Then I met Zach and came to work at The Plaza."

Beth pushed the finished centerpiece aside and glanced down at her watch. "I think I'll make it. Our pro-life group meets tonight at St. Agnes Church."

"Are you Catholic?" Sammy asked.

"No, I'm Presbyterian. My father was a minister, but he's retired now. Had some health problems. But he always taught me to try and make a difference. To get involved. Do you believe that?"

"I never thought much about it. Maybe because my life has been anything but normal."

"Why's that?" Beth asked.

"My mom died when I was twelve, and I never knew my father. So I went to St. Joseph's Home until I was adopted by a family in White Chapel.

The woman who adopted me was born in Sweden. Her name's Legna."

"What about the man who adopted you? Your father?"

Sammy stared at Beth, and wondered what he should tell her about Max. "He wasn't a good father." He paused. "There's more ... none of it pleasant."

"Don't you believe that everything happens for a reason? Sometimes we don't know why, but we usually end up where we're meant to be."

"How about you. Are you where you're meant to be?" Sammy asked.

"I think so."

"And how did you get involved with pro-life?"

Beth was quiet, with the light from the chandelier playing with strands of her blonde hair. Her eyes then grew wide, and Sammy got lost in their blueness. "I don't tell many people," she said, "but I thought about joining the Sisters of Charity when I got out of school. But then decided to go to college and work in social services. And now I'm at The Plaza. It's like I'm supposed to be here and be helping out at the shelter."

"Where's the shelter?"

"It's on Fourth Street, and it's called *Room at the Inn.* If you'd like to volunteer, we always need help moving furniture or putting a crib together."

"I live close by. I'm on First Street, and I'd be glad to help."

Beth slid a fern into the centerpiece and spoke without looking up. "When you work here, you never know what you'll have to do to keep the hotel going. One night, when one of the chefs called off sick, I was in the kitchen peeling hundreds of shrimp. Today, I'm a florist." Then holding the last centerpiece in her hands, Beth placed it in the middle of the table. "The Harris Banquet has been saved, and let's call it a night."

Beth walked toward the door and Sammy followed. After she turned off the lights, darkness swelled the banquet room. Standing next to Beth in the pitch black room, Sammy's palms felt moist and his uniforms, sealed in plastic, felt slippery in his hands. And even though they had just met, how could he explain his heart pounding in his chest?

Walking out into the cool night air, Beth led Sammy through the parking lot to a powder blue convertible.

"Nice car," Sammy said. Leaning down, he glanced inside at the leather seats and plush carpet. The neatness and style of the car suited Beth. He could imagine her driving through town, her mane of blonde hair tossing about her face, and how everyone, especially the men, would take notice.

An awkward silence followed. Then Beth reached into her purse and dangled a ring of keys from her hands. For a time no one spoke, and only the drone of the hotel's cooling system, swirling steel blades with a steady hum, filled the night.

Beth then moved closer to Sammy. "I'll let you know when we need help at the shelter. And thanks for your company tonight."

Sammy nodded, and Beth got into her car. As he watched her powder blue car disappear from sight, he felt a dull ache in his heart — a feeling he had never felt before. Could he ever have a relationship with Beth? Could he have a relationship with anyone?

If he did, he would be living a lie.

Chapter 18

Legna began each night as she began each morning — reading Scripture. And after reading Psalm 21: 8, she wondered why she chose that verse.

"Thine hand shall find all thy enemies: thy right hand shall find those that hate thee."

Setting the Bible down on the nightstand, she picked up the envelope that had been delivered today. The outside of the envelope was printed with block letters and addressed to the Swinehauser Family. Postmarked from Pittsburgh, it had no return address and was sealed with scotch tape. When Legna opened the letter, the same block print appeared on jagged-edged paper that looked as if it had been torn from a notebook. There were only two sentences:

I KNOW WHAT YOU DID. YOU WON'T GET
AWAY WITH IT.

As Legna held the letter in her hand, she
wondered if she should call Detective DeLuca, who
was investigating Max's disappearance? And should
she tell Sammy? There was no way to trace an
anonymous letter. *Or was there?* Legna held the
letter to her nose, and a sweet scent rose from the
lined paper. Everyone had their own fragrance, their
own scent, and it was not an unfamiliar smell
encased in the paper.

She placed the letter on the nightstand, next to
the framed picture of Max. He stood in the front
yard holding a bottle of Mr. Bud Cola, and wearing
the flannel hunting jacket he got for his birthday.
But since Max disappeared, even the white frame
house was not the same. Like a friend, the home had
grown with Legna, and she knew every grained and
weathered board. Now strange noises came from the
basement at night. But when she crept down the

basement stairs, with the rifle by her side, only a field mouse darted past and jumped up onto the rafters. And last night, while sitting out on the back porch, Legna heard someone in the woods behind the house. They were not sounds made by an animal, but were human feet stirring through the brush. Yet when she ventured into the woods in the dead of night, she found nothing as she stood enveloped by trees with the Remington rifle cocked and ready to fire.

Legna pulled back the covers and gazed at a room submerged in moonlight. She had not drawn the blinds, and the wood floor appeared as if covered with slats of gold. The velvet chair in the corner, bathed in moonlight, seemed raised from the fabric. And her red jacket, hanging over the back of the chair, appeared as a fireball of light. Legna held onto the wood post and raised herself from the bed. Standing in the center of the room, straight and erect, she cast a shadow over the carpet of moonlight. Legna then stared at the clock. The hour was 3:00

A.M. The house was dark, but she knew her steps in the night. Walking down the stairs, Legna went to the sitting room and sank into an armchair. Surrounded by silence, everything was still; and Legna could only hear her heart beating, which kept time with the grandfather clock. Only sounds of the night filled the house — nothing to have Legna toting the rifle from room to room in search of unexplained noises.

Resting her head against the back of the chair, she folded her hands and began to pray. *"Please God, protect our family from those who want to harm us. Keep evil away and surround us with your love."* Legna felt a calm settle over her. She had no fear.

She felt God beside her.

The sun warmed the morning air as Legna walked down the road to Sally Fletcher's house. Inhaling the sweet smell of fall, leaves crunched underfoot as she passed naked trees that gave deep shade in the summer. When she reached Sally's house, evergreens circled the brick ranch that was set back from the road. Glancing down at the lawn, glistening under a net of dew, Legna could almost hear laughter and see Sally's six children playing in the yard. She then remembered how Sally would come into the yard and arrange the children around her skirt as if arranging flowers in a vase.

Legna stepped onto the porch, scattering the family of cats that made there home there. When Sally greeted her, the house held the scent of a cherry-wood fire, and Sally's hair normally tamed into a bun, curled around her face like strands of gray twisted wire. Legna followed behind as Sally led her to a room with celery-colored furniture and a rug so thick and green it was like wading through grass. Taking a seat on the couch, Legna glanced at pictures on the wall of Sally's late husband, Chester, and her grandchildren.

"How many grandchildren do you have now?" Legna asked.

"God Bless. We have twelve. Eight boys and four girls."

"I always wanted a brood of kids. But maybe someday I'll have some grandchildren."

"I'm sure you will." Sally paused. "Tell me, how's Sammy doing?"

"He's a chef at The Plaza Hotel and loves his job."

Then there was silence. "Any … any word about Max?" Sally asked.

"No. None."

"How are you managing," Sally asked, "and have you thought about moving?"

"I'll never move. After Max went missing, his cousin Charlie from California called me. He wanted to buy the house, but I told him I could never move. I can't imagine living anywhere else."

Raising a veined hand, Sally began to fumble with the button on the collar of her blouse.

"You know Max's cousin, Charlie, was in town. He came to see me," Sally said. "Wants to come back to Pennsylvania and buy some property here. Said he's tired of California."

"I didn't know he was in town. Wonder why he didn't stop by to see me?"

"Cause he thinks Sammy had something to do with Max's disappearance," Sally blurted out. "Charlie knew they never got along." She then sat back and sighed. "I'm sorry. I shouldn't have said that."

Legna could feel her cheeks redden as she locked eyes with Sally. "Charlie's mistaken. Sammy would never do anything to harm anyone."

"I know dear. I should never have mentioned Charlie. He even went to Pittsburgh to see somebody by the name of Detective DeLuca; he's handling Max's disappearance. The detective told Charlie he thinks the sheriff had something to do with Max being missing. Something about they were taking money from the state. Cremating prisoners."

"I know all about that. But can't imagine the sheriff doing anything to harm Max."

"Don't know. Don't know if we'll ever know what happened," Sally said.

"Is Charlie still in town?" Legna asked.

Sally hesitated. " I ... I really don't know."

As Legna watched Sally's pale tight face and unsteady hands, she remembered how frail she had become since her husband died. For weeks after his death, the blinds were drawn and the house remained dark. And when Sally tried to speak, her words came out jumbled. Yet Legna's words were slow, but steady when she spoke. "I don't want to upset you, but you should know some strange things have been happening. I've been hearing noises in the basement and in the woods behind my house."

"Wonder if they ever found out who was breaking into the homes here awhile back?" Sally asked. "Bet it's that crazy Otis, the man who prowls around at all hours of the night. Saw him one time behind the house. Probably trying to peek in my windows."

"I don't think Otis is behind the break-ins. Whoever is, I have my rifle. And I'm not afraid to use it."

"Goodness ... just be careful," Sally said. "And be sure to keep your doors locked."

Legna crossed the room and walked toward the door. "You need to be careful, too. Living here all by yourself. And don't worry about me, I'll be just fine."

As Legna trudged home, a solitary cloud formed overhead, perfectly shaped and edged in sunlight. Yet the sun offered little comfort, little warmth, and Legna moved her feet slowly along the gravel road, turning to stare at each car that drove by.

When she reached her house, Legna's eyes drifted to the front yard and the birch tree, with layers of peeling bark. From a branch overhead, a black crow peered down and let out a haunting squawk. The crow then took flight, soaring higher and higher until it appeared as a black speck in the sky. Dragging herself up the porch stairs, Legna went inside, locked the deadbolt, and closed the blinds. She lifted a corner of the blinds and peeked out. Then with her heart racing, she wondered who was trying to frighten her?

And why?

Chapter 19

When the orders in the hotel kitchen began to slow down, Sammy took his time garnishing a platter of chicken with sprigs of parsley. Luke, the chef working beside him, stood assembling a ham sandwich for Zach, the hotel manager, positioning the lettuce and tomato perfectly on the wheat bread. No salt, no pepper, light on the mayo, and served with a cup of black coffee. This is how Zach liked his night-time snack, and each evening it was served by a busboy on a pewter tray. While working the late shift on Friday night, Zach could be found standing guard in the hotel lounge, in the middle of a cloud of cigarette smoke, as one of the local bands caused the walls and floors to pulsate.

Luke edged closer to Sammy. "We're getting together tonight in the lounge around 10:00. Why don't you join us?" he asked.

"I already have plans."

"Who you meeting?"

"Her name's Legna."

"Sounds like a dancer to me," Luke said.

"She's not a dancer. She's the woman who adopted me."

"Sure ... sure she is," Luke said, raising his thick brows.

Trying to hide a smile, Sammy placed his last order on the tray. He then scrubbed his hands, hung his jacket in his locker, and left the hotel. A flash of neon lights brought a darkened city to life as he drove through town. When he stopped at the traffic light on Second Street, he gazed at a maroon building on the corner that was for sale. It was sturdy, all brick, and may have once been a restaurant with an outside area where customers would have dined. The three apartments above the main floor appeared vacant. As he stared at the brick building, Sammy imagined himself inside, cooking for a packed house while a hostess escorted customers to their table. There was something about the building — something that made him jot down the name and phone number of the realtor handling the sale. He could even see the name of his restaurant on the blank sign above the door. He would call it *Legna's Place.*

As Sammy drove from the city, the lights of town faded into a wall of trees that lined the road toward White Chapel. The wall of trees was soon replaced by cornfields and the flicker of candles, glowing from farmhouse windows dotting the countryside. When Sammy turned onto Red Oak Lane, Legna's white-framed house appeared a pale blue in the moonlight. But darkness consumed the home, except for a lantern shining from the front window. Sammy fumbled for his key, unlocked the door, and went inside. When he walked toward the sitting room, he stepped on the raised wood at the base of the stairs, and it gave a squeal of protest. But as he stepped off the board, he froze. Aimed right at him was the barrel of a rifle.

"What … what are you doing?" Sammy hollered.

Legna's hands trembled as she lowered the butt of the rifle to the floor and gripped the barrel. "I didn't know you were coming tonight."

"I wanted to surprise you, but what's going on?"

Legna said nothing as she walked over to the fireplace and hung the rifle back on the rack. She then collapsed onto the couch. "I didn't want to burden you with this. You starting a new job and all. Just sit down here, there's some things I have to tell you."

"You have to tell me everything."

"I don't know where to begin, and I don't know what's going on. The other night I was out back sitting on the porch, and I heard noises coming from the woods. Someone moving about in the brush. And another night, there were sounds coming from the basement. Like someone was dragging their feet across the floor."

"When did this all start?"

"A few weeks ago."

"There were break-ins around here a while back. Maybe you should come stay with me at my apartment."

Legna was quiet, twirling a lock of faded auburn hair around her fingers. "I'm not going anywhere." She paused. "It's Charlie. I know it's him."

"He *was* in town. Came to see me at The Plaza, and looks just like Max. Only older."

"You never told me. Why would he come to see you?"

"He came here to look for Max. Said he has his suspicions."

"He can have all the suspicion he wants. What Charlie wants is my property. He's trying to scare me off, but it won't work."

Legna walked over to the desk and took an envelope from the drawer. When she handed it to Sammy, he read the jagged-edged note inside.

"What does this mean? *I know what you did. You won't get away with it.* I don't understand any of this."

"Nobody's going to run me off, and I'm not going anywhere," Legna said.

"If you won't come and stay with me, I'm calling Sally Fletcher. Have her come by and check on you. And keep your doors locked, especially the deadbolt."

"You're not to worry. I'm a tough Swede." The lines around Legna's eyes softened, as they did each time a smile crossed her face. "I share a history with this house. There were good times here with Max. Wrote about them in my book." Legna hesitated. "You know, I finished my memoir. I have it in the metal chest in the closet. It's my gift to you after I pass on. It's the story of my life."

Sammy then watched Legna curl up on the couch, and she appeared child-like, more fragile than he could remember. With his eyes on Legna, an ache filled his heart, the same ache he felt when he was twelve years old and his mother died. And he often wondered if it was misfortune or fate that brought Legna into his life?

Legna sat up and rested her head against the back of the couch. "You know, I always tried my best with Max. But I tried to make Max into someone he could never be. Because there was something inside Max, like a flaw in a diamond, something not visible to the naked eye that I couldn't change. And there's some other things you need to know. All the important papers are in the metal chest in my closet. My will. Everything. And I want to be buried, no cremation. And when I do pass away, you're not to worry. You'll be well taken care of."

With a mix of emotions, Sammy tried to steady his voice. "Now, remember what you said. You're a tough Swede, and you're not going anywhere."

Chapter 20

Sammy stared back at his image in the mirror. His reflection revealed a tall, broad-shouldered man with dark hair and eyes. As he stared at his reflection, he thought he must resemble his father, a man he never knew. He then wondered if he ever passed his father on the street, or had his father ever searched for him? Or was he even aware he had a son? But Sammy pushed the thought from his mind. Today was Saturday, almost noon, and he was going to help Beth at the shelter.

When Sammy arrived at the shelter, the turn-of-the-century building displayed a grand style of architecture, with raised columns at each end of the brick building and a cement design stamped around each window. When he knocked on the door, a nun veiled in black answered.

"Good morning. I've come to help Beth."

The full-skirted nun led him inside, and the building held a chill as they walked down a hallway covered with curled blocks of green linoleum. When they passed a room crammed full of mismatched chairs and mattresses, she hurried and closed the door. "That's our storage room," she said. "Excuse the mess." She then led Sammy to an apartment with high ceilings, pale yellow walls, and a chair oozing its stuffing that sat next to a gas fireplace. A window, which almost reached the ceiling, drew the city inside and framed a view of the steel mill across the river. As clouds formed overhead, puffs of smoke billowed from the mill's metal stacks and blended into a gray Pittsburgh sky.

Sammy turned when Beth entered the room. Dressed in snug jeans and a t-shirt, her hair was pulled back into a ponytail, that swayed from side to side when she walked.

"So glad you came," she said, squeezing her hands into the pockets of her jeans.

For a moment, he stood studying Beth's face as if admiring a painting. She wore a trace of pink lipstick, a sweep of blush on her cheeks, and light from the window made a cluster of gold flecks dance inside her pale blue eyes. With his eyes on Beth, his voice echoed through the sparsely furnished room. "Where's the crib you need assembled?"

Beth led him to a small room in the back of the apartment. "This is the nursery. Hope you can put this all together," she said, staring down at the nuts, bolts, and sections of a crib scattered across the floor. "There's a hammer and whatever else you need in the tool box. Holler if you need anything."

As Sammy began screwing bolts into the wood frame, a crib soon began to take shape. For an instant, his mind began to wander … Sammy imagined he and Beth were married, and he was putting the crib together for their child, a baby girl who would have wisps of blonde hair and enormous blue eyes like Beth.

The squeal of a screw, grinding into the leg of the crib, brought Sammy back to reality. He then stood back and admired the crib with almost a reverence. The crib, with carved oak spindles, would hold a tiny infant, a baby a mother chose to keep and love.

After putting the tools away, Sammy paced around the apartment which needed curtains to soften the windows, rugs for the wood floor, and pictures for walls the color of sunlight. But aside from what the apartment needed, he felt a warmth in the stark, bare rooms with radiators that hissed to their own tune. And there seemed to be a presence here. Was it the nuns, filled with peace and love, who spread joy in each room they entered? Or was it a presence that is revealed when you do the will of God?

As Sammy glanced out the window, Beth came and stood beside him. Together, they stared out at the steel mill as a hush fell over the room which could have suited a monastery. Beth said nothing, and gazed out at smoke billowing from the metal stacks as if she never had occasion to see it before.

Sammy broke the silence. "What did you think of the crib?"

"It's beginning to look like a nursery."

"When's the baby due?" Sammy asked.

"Amy had her baby. She had a little girl, and we have to get busy. We still need things for the apartment. Like some rugs. Curtains. Maybe some pictures for the walls."

"I'm sure the woman who adopted me would have things to donate. I told you about her. Her name's Legna."

"That's such an unusual name," Beth said.

"She's from Sweden. And it's angel spelled backward."

"We'll take any donations, especially from an angel."

Sammy smiled to himself. He would come back with boxes of housewares. And using the donated goods as a ruse, he would see Beth another Saturday.

Sammy glanced at his watch. "How about some lunch?" he asked. "There's a café up the street, and we'll pass a restaurant that's for sale. It has a great location."

"I am a little hungry. But I can't be gone for long."

Walking against a skyline of buildings, they blended in with people moving up and down the sidewalk and shoppers milling from store to store. When they rounded the corner, they passed a man peddling flowers and pushing a cart with a limp green awning.

"Roses here," he chanted, as he went by. "Not twenty … not fifteen. Not even ten. Only five dollars a dozen. How 'bout some for your pretty lady?"

Beth blushed and color flooded her cheeks.

"No … no thanks," Sammy said.

With Beth's cheeks tinged in red, they elbowed their way through a crowd boarding a trolley. But when a tractor trailer barreled down the street, it left Beth's hair swirling around her face and the metal grate they were standing on shaking beneath their feet. After walking a short distance, they followed a brick sidewalk that led them to the building that was for sale. Sammy peered inside the glass store front where a *For Sale* sign hung from the window.

"What do you think?" Sammy asked.

Beth stepped back and glanced up at the four-story building. "It's all brick. Has a good location, and the apartments look empty. You know, we could use more space for our mothers at the shelter. But ... can you afford to buy it?"

"Probably not. But there's something about this building, something I can't explain."

Sammy turned around and stared back at the building before they entered the Diamond Café. After sitting in a corner booth, a young woman with red cropped hair and a skinny black skirt came and dabbed at their table with a wet cloth. She smiled as she laid the menus down on the table. "Today's special is the Rueben sandwich," she said, before drifting off to another table.

"You know, they have a great pastrami sandwich," Sammy said.

"I think I'll have tuna on whole wheat," Beth said, glancing down at the menu.

"You know, other than you like tuna, I don't know much about you."

"What would you like to know?"

Sammy hesitated. He wanted to know all about Beth, from what she experienced as a child to everything she had done in her life, but only replied, "Tell me whatever you like."

"I grew up in Philadelphia, where my parents still live ... have an older sister. You know my father's a retired minister. And that I worked in social services a few years. Then I came to The Plaza. And oh, I forgot about Sampson."

"Who's that?" Sammy asked.

"He's my cat. Sampson's black with emerald green eyes and looks like a small black panther. Weighs only about five pounds, but he feels powerful. So I gave him a powerful name."

Sammy forced a smile, thinking of the black panther that lurked in his dreams with green eyes that flashed in the night. But his attention turned to the waitress, who came and set their order down on the table.

Beth tapped a packet of sugar into her iced tea and spoke between bites of her sandwich. "That's enough about me. I know you lost your mother and went to live at St. Joseph's Home. What was it like there?"

"It wasn't so bad. We had a priest who was like my father. His name was Father John. Then you know, I was adopted."

"And the man who adopted you. You said you didn't have a good relationship with him growing up. Have things gotten any better?"

Sammy could feel his throat tighten, and the words came out slow. "He … he's gone missing. Been missing about five years now."

"How strange to just vanish. Disappear. Wonder what happened to him?"

Sammy lowered his head, and in his mind, the crowded café grew silent awaiting his reply. When he looked up, he caught Beth's stare and pushed his plate aside. He then stood up, reached into his pocket and tossed a five dollar tip on the table.

"I ... know you have to get back," he said. "We better get going."

When they left the café, they became part of a group exiting the matinee at the Regency Theater. After weaving through the crowd, Beth stopped to gaze at storefronts with mannequins dressed in fashions for the season.

As they stood waiting for the traffic light to change, and without any sign of a breeze, a stinging wind ripe from the river jabbed at Sammy's face like a fork. Then memories clouded his mind, thoughts that had their own color, taste, and sound. And even though the sun was shining, a darkness consumed him.

The memory of Max refused to die.

Chapter 21

Legna held the pamphlet the doctor gave her with COPD, chronic obstructive pulmonary disease, printed on the cover — another ailment in addition to high blood pressure, diabetes, and an irregular heartbeat. Palpitations plagued her; and when kneeling down to pray, she found it hard not to remain there forever. And though the weather was warm, when winter arrived even layers of flannel covering up worn joints would not relieve the creaking and aching in her bones. She leaned back in the chair, but her thoughts were interrupted when the doorbell chimed. When Legna pulled back the drapes her neighbor, Sally Fletcher, stood on the porch.

"God bless, and here's something for you," Sally said, handing Legna a silver gift bag, spilling over with tissue paper and *Happy Birthday* scripted on the front.

"How nice of you," Legna said. "Come in. Please."

When they sat down on the couch, Sally moved closer to Legna. "I love your dress with the flowers and all. You know, I used to have wallpaper just like it." Sally paused. "Now go on and open your gift. I use it all the time, and you can only buy it at Phil's Pharmacy."

Legna reached inside the bag and peeled back tissue from a bottle of hand lotion. She unscrewed the cap and smelled the lotion that held a scent of fresh vanilla. She then held it closer to her nose.

"Excuse me a minute," Legna said. Walking into her bedroom, she took out the letter written on the lined note paper that came last week. She smelled the letter. She smelled it again. Putting it back into the envelope, Legna slipped it inside the front of her blouse. She then came back into the room and sat down.

"I have to ask you something. Why did you do it? Why did you send me this letter?" Legna asked, pulling the letter out from the front of her blouse.

Sally's face turned purple. Then red.

"I ... didn't mean no harm. Charlie made me do it. He wanted to scare you off so he could buy your house. Be close to me, help me. When he was here, he cleaned out the shed and got rid of all that rotted wood along side the house. He even painted the kitchen. Do you know how hard it's been since Chester died?"

Legna sat back, drew in her breath, and tried to steady her voice. "I don't understand how you could do this? You go to mass every Sunday, but what you really need to do is stay away from Charlie."

"He went back to California. Don't even know if he's coming back," Sally said.

"You still have the key to my house. Don't you?" Legna asked.

Sally took out the keys from her pocket and began fingering through them with hands, thin and translucent as onion skins.

"I should have it," she said, sorting through the keys again. Sally then set down the keys and let out a deep sigh. "I don't understand. Had it right there on that ring."

"I hope Charlie didn't take the key to my house," Legna said.

"He knew I had it. Asked me one day about the gold key on the ring. All the others were silver. Now it's gone."

"The noises I heard in the woods and in my basement. Always thought it was Charlie. Let himself in the back door with my key and was trying to run me off."

Sally's bottom lip quivered and her eyes welled with tears. "I'm sorry," she said, between sobs. "Don't know why I went along with Charlie. I didn't mean to hurt you."

Legna patted Sally's shoulders that shook with each sob. Then with her hands covering her face, Sally began to whimper so softly her cries could barely be heard.

"Now, now … don't cry," Legna said, in a slow soothing voice. "Sometimes you can't see evil, and you can be deceived. We've been friends a long time, and you just made a mistake."

"Hope you can forgive me. You've had enough heartache with Max being gone." Sally gazed up with apple cheeks, a little pointed chin, and eyes still large and caramel-colored. Then she retreated into quiet; and for a moment, her face appeared as if encased in ice. Expressionless.

But when Sally spoke, her voice rose high and shrill. "I know people talk behind my back. They call me a gossip and an old biddy. Charlie made me feel young again, but I was foolish. Lonely and foolish."

Sally stood, zipped her open jacket, and hobbled to the door. The woman who drank far too much coffee and talked more than people wished she would, seemed even smaller as Legna watched her retreat back to her house with her arms cemented to her sides.

Legna then went to the drawer, took out the phone book and dialed a number.

"A & M Locksmith," the voice answered on the other end.

"Hello, I need to have some locks changed. Can you please send someone out to 1130 Red Oak Lane in White Chapel?"

Chapter 22

Legna glanced at the flame of the candle that straightened, bent, then cast a halo of light on the dining room ceiling of The Plaza Hotel. The collar of her turquoise dress, sewn with rows of sequins, glittered and sparkled from the light. Yet as she sat at a table, laden with fine silverware and crisp white linens, her eyes were on Sammy. Dressed in a charcoal suit, he studied the menu with his head down and strands of dark hair falling across his forehead. When he glanced up, he caught Legna's stare.

"I can't think of a better way to spend your birthday," he said. "That's why I took the day off. We need to celebrate."

The candlelight softened the lines on Legna's face as she leaned closer to Sammy. "I'm having a great time, but before I forget," she said reaching

172

into her purse, "here's a new key to the house. I got the locks changed."

"Why did you get them changed?"

"I don't know if you would understand. But I believe any woman can be led astray by a man."

"And what does that have to do with you changing the locks?"

"Sally and I have been friends for a long time. Let's just say it's a woman thing."

"Must be, and I'll never understand women. All I understand is food. And by the way, I recommend the chicken cordon bleu."

"Good choice," a soft voice answered. And when Sammy looked up, Beth was standing by the table.

"Hey, what are you doing here?" Sammy asked.

"They needed linens brought down and all the busboys were busy."

Sammy nodded. "Beth, I'd like you to meet Legna." He hesitated, searching for words to describe the woman who changed his life. "Legna became my second mother after my mother died. And today we're celebrating her birthday."

Legna smiled when Beth extended her hand. "Nice to meet you, and Happy Birthday."

"Why don't you join us?" Sammy asked.

"I have to get back, but I'll see you tomorrow. We need to go over the Weaver Convention for next week. We have a big group coming."

Beth turned to Legna. "Enjoy your birthday, and it was nice meeting you."

When Beth walked toward the door, she passed four men seated at the next table, and eight eyes followed her until she was out of sight. As Sammy glared at the men, he could feel his jaw tighten.

"You have feelings for Beth, don't you?" Legna asked.

"We're just friends. Neither of us want a relationship right now."

She's sweet on you. I can tell. Beth looks at you like Max looked at me when we were courting. A woman knows these things."

"The only thing I want to know is how your doctor's appointment went last week. Is everything all right?"

Legna swallowed hard to hold back her cough. "You know I'd tell you if anything was wrong. Dr. Watkins said everything is fine. Everything's just fine," Legna said, burying her head in the menu.

When Sammy arrived at Beth's office the next day, he leafed through the orders for the Weaver Convention. "We can start serving at 7:00," he said, to Beth "but we may need help, this is a big convention."

"I know, I'll talk to Zach in the morning." Beth then began gathering up papers on her desk and stacking them into a pile. "And how was lunch with Legna?"

"Nice. She had a great birthday. And how are things going with you? How are things at the shelter?"

"Busy. We're always busy. And I meant to tell you, I passed the building on Second Street you were looking at. You know, it's still for sale."

"They're asking $82,000 for it. That's a lot of money. I did go through the building with the realtor. The kitchen and dining room are in decent shape, but the apartments need some work."

As Sammy walked toward the door, he could see a tall figure through the frosted glass. After a knock on the door, Joel entered. Reeking with the smell of aftershave, he edged closer to Beth.

"Hey Joel," Beth said. "I just need to finish up a few things and we'll get started on the signs. We're expecting a huge rally at the courthouse on Saturday."

"You know me ... always willing to lend a hand." Joel then stood next to Sammy and spoke in a hushed tone. "Did I hear you say you were leaving?"

With a slam of the door, Sammy left Beth's office. He then wandered down to the lobby where scents from the Teapot Café lured him inside. He sat down at the counter next to a woman with a cloud of white well-tended hair, who seemed to be humming to a tune only she could hear. Wedged on the stool, she meticulously slathered butter onto a roll, soft and plump as the flesh under her arms. "Try the sirloin steak," she said. "So tender you can cut it with a fork. My name's Hilda. I live in the high-rise on Fifth Avenue. Always treat myself to dinner on Friday."

Sammy nodded and forced a smile.

"I grew up not far from here, on the South Side. Dad was a tailor and Mom stayed home and took care of eight kids. We were poor, but we didn't know it. We were happy." She patted her mouth with the napkin, and then directed her gaze at Sammy.

"You look like something's wrong? Did you break-up with your girlfriend? Or has someone died?"

"No … nothing like that."

"You know my Edgar died last year. We were married fifty years. I was so depressed after he died, but then I could hear him saying, 'Hilda, you have to get over things.' He would always tell me that. And he …," she stopped mid-sentence when the waitress placed a menu in front of Sammy.

"Sorry to keep you waiting, but we're so busy tonight," the waitress said.

"I know you're busy, dear, but you don't want to keep this nice young man waiting."

Sammy picked up the menu, but said nothing. As he sat in the crowded café, thoughts of Beth and his life of deception played out in his mind. Lowering his head, feelings of guilt, feelings that could emerge at any time clouded his mind.

Sammy then glanced at the woman seated beside him. She had called him a nice young man. But what would she think, and what would Beth think, if they knew he had taken a life?

Chapter 23

On the day of the pro-life rally, the courthouse swarmed with men and woman who stood shoulder to shoulder in front of the century-old building. Some carried signs with a message supporting life, and many held signs with a picture of a chubby-cheeked baby and a caption that read: *Thank you for letting me live.*

Sammy's eyes traveled to the entrance of the courthouse, searching for Beth. But with so many people attending the rally, he could not find her. He squeezed into an empty space on a bench, next to a woman who fumbled through a shoulder bag, as large as a bed pillow. A little girl, with a mass of curls, sat fidgeting beside her. The woman zipped the leather bag and glanced up at Sammy.

"Never saw you at a rally before. Are you a member of our group?" she asked.

"I don't belong to any group. But I believe in the cause."

"I'm a single mom, and this is my daughter, Emma." She stopped to stare at the little girl with eyes the color of green marbles. "She's been a handful, but I don't know what I'd do without her. She took the little girl's hand and they walked up the steps of the courthouse. The woman then picked up a sign, and the little girl clasped tiny fingers around a small sign that read *My Mother Chose Life*.

But everyone stopped marching when a priest came up to the podium. Sammy moved closer when he realized the priest was Father John from St. Joseph's Home. He was still lean, his hair now peppered with gray, and he still had a glint in his eyes that was visible even from a distance. The crowd quieted when Father John began to speak.

"It's been said history will repeat itself." Father John paused. "But we can also learn from history. On this very ground we stand, more than a hundred years ago, Christians may have gathered to voice their concerns for another group who had no rights. They were held hostage, in bondage, like a piece of property. We all know these people were slaves. And as we come together today, I see similarities in our struggle."

A mother carrying an infant walked up to the podium and handed her baby to Father John. He stood staring down at the baby who squirmed in his arms. "If you want to see God, look into the eyes of a child. You'll see love, and you'll see God. So as we gather here today, let's all see life through the eyes of God."

After Father John spoke, the crowd cheered and the applause was deafening. Sammy tried to press through the crowd, but when he reached the podium, Father John was nowhere in sight. He then found himself in the center of the group, and being swept into the tide of men and women carrying a sign.

"Hey buddy," a man said to him. "Here, take this," and he shoved a sign into his hands. Then

Sammy found himself marching, moving with the group and holding the sign high in the air. As he became part of the group, for an instant the darkness that consumed him, day and night, was replaced by peace.

The next day when Sammy arrived at the hotel kitchen, he scrubbed his hands like a doctor preparing for surgery and slipped on a white jacket. Taking his place at his workstation, he stared down at the griddle. "What's this? It's the second time this week," he said, peering down at a heart-shaped pancake.

Luke, the chef beside him, inched closer. "Must be Cynthia," he said. "I should have warned you about her."

Sammy's eyes circled the kitchen for the shy young woman with a tense smile, but she was nowhere in sight.

"Be careful," Luke said. "Cynthia takes a liking to all the new chefs. And if you just smile at her, it's like that was your first date."

Sammy gave Luke a side-glance, flipped the pancake into the trash, and reached above his head for the breakfast orders. "Wonder how many omelets we'll have for today?"

"Don't know," Luke said, "but Zach wants a western omelet with lots of green peppers. I almost have it ready."

"Want me to take it up for you?" Sammy asked.

"Hoping you would. And you know Zach *has* to have it on his pewter tray."

Sammy placed the omelet, two buttered slices of wheat toast, and a scalding cup of black coffee on the tray. With the meal in hand, he walked down the white-marbled hallway that appeared as a gold speckled sheet of ice. He stopped when he came to the end of the hall and the door with *Hotel Manager* scripted across a metal bar.

When Sammy entered, Zach sat behind a large mahogany desk with an ashtray spilling over with cigarette butts. He rose from his desk as sunlight painted a shine on his gold-capped tooth. "How's it going?" he asked. "I didn't expect you to bring up my breakfast."

"I'm helping out Luke."

"You know I've been wanting to tell you, I've been hearing good things about you. Hope you stay on with us. So many chefs try to go out on their own. Believe me, I've been in the restaurant business for years, and it's a tough business."

Sammy nodded in agreement, but he once pictured Zach as a man who would take on any challenge. But years seemed to erase the fight from his face. A square jaw now hung more relaxed, half-moon pouches rested under his hazel eyes, and his lips appeared as if drawn into a straight line.

"I couldn't afford my own place," Sammy said, as Zach bit into a slice of toast. "Besides, I like working here. I've made some good friends, and I'm not planning on leaving. Well … guess I better get back."

Walking past the lobby, Sammy stopped when he came to Beth's office. As he peered through the frosted glass, he saw her seated at her desk. He knocked on the door, and when she answered, her head was drawn down.

"Everything all right? I missed you at the rally on Saturday."

Beth stood with her chin trembling and her eyes clouded by tears. "I couldn't make it. Had to go to Philadelphia. My father, he passed away."

"I'm … I'm sorry. What happened?"

"He hadn't been in good health, and his heart just gave out." With a rush of tears, Beth began to sob — sobs that tore at Sammy's heart.

Sammy moved closer and wanted to comfort her. Soothe her. And it seemed natural when he pulled Beth close to his chest. Then with his arms wrapped around her, he closed his eyes and held her as though she were a piece of fine china, fragile, afraid she may shatter at any moment. Drifting off to another place, he became lost in the softness of her shoulders and the sweet scent laced through her hair.

Afraid to speak, Sammy spoke in a hushed tone.

"I know ... I know," was all he could think to say.

Beth slipped out from under Sammy's arms. "I'm sorry," she said, dabbing her eyes with a tissue. "I don't know what came over me. I'll be all right." Blinking back tears, Beth sat down at her desk where tissues were balled like crumpled white roses. Her face, pale and streaked with tears, was a face not accustom to sadness.

Sammy was the first to speak. "Guess you heard about the rally. They had a big crowd, and you won't believe what happened. I marched and even carried a sign."

"How did that happen?"

"I tried to get through the crowd to see Father John. He's the priest from St. Joseph's Home who spoke at the rally. But the next thing you know, I was part of the group and marching along with them."

"We're having a rally at the courthouse every Saturday this month," Beth said. "If you can, try to come by. We need all the support we can get."

As Sammy held Beth's gaze, he thought of Zach's words. 'Unless you want to carry a sign for Beth, she wants nothing to do with men.'

But Sammy knew he could never be with the woman he thought of day and night. And he knew the reason why.

Chapter 24

Late day sun painted the oak walls a warm brown as Legna filled the bowls with chicken soup. When she set the ladle down, the soup bowls passed from hand to hand. A blue linen cloth draped the dining room table, and Legna had set out the china that belonged to her mother, ivory plates and bowls, swirled on the edges with bands of gold. But Legna, who was always a mountain of chatter, seemed quiet. Her auburn hair, pulled tight from her face, made the lines around her eyes appear deeper and her cheekbones more prominent than Sammy could remember. She sat down at the table and turned to Sammy.

"Guess you've been busy at the hotel." Legna paused. "And how are things with you and Beth.

Someday you both are going to be together. I just know it."

"We're friends. That's all. Just friends."

"Wish you would settle down and get married. So I could have some grandbabies."

Sammy adjusted the collar of his shirt in a room that seemed as hot as the soup. But when Legna spooned the broth, her hands shook and the soup spilled back onto the plate. She then set down her spoon and began to cough — a cough that rattled her chest and made her shoulders rigid.

"That cough doesn't seem to be getting any better. You need to go back and see Dr. Watkins."

"It's just a stubborn cold. I always get one this time of year." Legna lifted the napkin from a plate of biscuits. "Try a roll," she said. "They're homemade. I added a cup of mashed potatoes to the dough and it makes them nice and moist."

"I'm more worried about your cough. I may have to take you to see Dr. Watkins like *you* dragged me to see him when I was a boy."

"I'm fine. You're not to worry."

Legna stood up from her chair and Sammy followed behind. Walking into the sitting room, they sat on the patriotic couch with flags that appeared to be blowing in the wind.

"You can't get rid of this couch. Can you?" Sammy asked.

"Max loved this couch with the flags and all. Maybe because his birthday was the Fourth of July, like yours." Legna sighed. "You know, I think of Max all the time. Oh ... how I miss him. But we have little control over what happens in life."

Legna's words made Sammy think of his own life. How Legna rescued him after his mother died and how she tried to protect him from Max. Yet no one spoke as they watched the embers of a fire die out with the Remington rifle guarding the house from the rack above the fireplace. Everything was still, quiet, with only the pendulum of the grandfather clock swinging from behind its wall of glass.

"You know, it's getting late," Sammy said. "I better get back." When Sammy wrapped his arms around Legna, he could feel the sharp edges of her spine, bone by bone. She appeared so thin, so fragile.

"You take care of yourself. And call Dr. Watkins about that cough."

Sammy left, and Legna climbed the stairs to her bedroom. Once in her room, she glanced down at the glass bottles lining her dresser. But she did not splash her face with rose water, as she did each night, or frame her hair with pink foam rollers. Slipping into her nightgown, she only wondered if tonight would be the night. In Sweden, a window is left open so the soul of the departed can ascend into heaven. Legna walked over to the window and pushed up the sash. As she gazed out into the dark, a slight wind ruffled leaves on the maple tree, the moon sparkled down from the heavens, and the air smelled like the woods after a rain. It was a perfect night to die.

Then getting back into bed, she lay in the same bed her mother and father had shared, the bed she had been born in and the bed she would die in. But Legna had no fear of death as the words to her favorite hymn played in her mind. She once read that John Newton, a slave trader, wrote *Amazing Grace* in the middle of a horrific storm. Did he feel as she did, that life was coming to an end? Legna began singing the words above a whisper.

Amazing Grace, how sweet the sound,

That saved a wretch like me ...

I once was lost but now am found,

Was blind, but now I see.

With her voice trailing into the darkness, Legna's eyes fluttered, then closed, and it seemed as if a dark curtain had been drawn around her bed.

When she wakened the next morning, the room held a chill, and she shivered under the blankets. Walking over to the window, she pulled down the sash with panes of glass covered in dew. It wasn't last night, but maybe it would be tonight. She would leave the window open.

Maybe it would be tonight.

Chapter 25

When the phone rang in the early morning, Sammy hesitated before picking up the receiver. The voice on the line was that of a woman who paused to sigh before she spoke. "God bless, this is Sally Fletcher. I'm so sorry ... but I have something terrible to tell you. Legna passed away. When I came to check on her this morning, I found her in bed. The window was wide open, and the room was like an icebox. Can't understand that, with her cough and all."

Sammy gripped the phone so tight, he thought it would break. He couldn't speak, yet he wanted to shout, pound his fists on his chest, but instead pulled his hand to his mouth and bit down hard.

"Are you still there?" Sally asked.

"I'm … I'm here," Sammy said, swallowing the knot in his throat.

"I know it's hard, but Legna had a peaceful death. She would have wanted it that way. She went to sleep and never awakened. And you know if you need anything at all, just call me." Her voice dropped and began to crack. "Let me know about the arrangements." Then there was silence. "You know … I'm really going to miss her."

Sammy's shoulders crumpled as he dragged himself to the couch. Then from deep inside came a primal cry — shrill and piercing — a cry that caused Sammy to tremble. He buried his face in his hands and began to sob, the same sobs he cried when he was twelve years old and his mother died. After wrung dry of tears, he sat rigid, unable to move. And in his darkness and despair, he did something he had not done in years, he cried out to God. *Please help me … Legna is gone, and I can't stand the pain.* Then with his face wet with tears, he prayed.

After Legna's funeral, Sammy tried to erase the pain and sorrow from his mind. He remembered how Beth stood beside him that day and squeezed his hand during the service, as if trying to give him strength. Zach and his friend, Luke, from The Plaza came along with Cynthia, who liked to make men heart-shaped pancakes. But how his heart ached each time he recalled the pearl-colored coffin being lowered into the ground, where the only living things that abided and dwelled were earthworms. Then the priest with his vestments flapping in the wind, read a verse which said faith in God claimed victory over death.

But as Sammy drove from Restland Cemetery after the funeral, he found no comfort in the priest's words — words which link the living to the dead. He felt hollow and empty inside. His heart was beating, yet he could barely feel it or feel himself breathing.

Because he was alive and Legna was dead.

When he drove through town, an afternoon shower pressed leaves against the wet brick streets. Driving past a row of buildings, with no destination in mind, he passed the building on Second Street that was for sale. A new sign, larger and in bold print, now hung from the window. But he did not park in front of the building, imagining himself inside cooking for a packed crowd. He could only think of Legna, the woman who no longer shared his life.

Sammy breathed in the sadness which was now a part of him as he drove toward Legna's house. Yet he dreaded going inside and not finding her there. Sensing his dread, the car Legna had bought for him seemed to think for him, seemed to have a mind of its own as it guided him toward White Chapel. With the car leading the way, Sammy turned onto Red Oak Lane. His steps were slow when he walked onto the front porch. Once inside the house, the walls seemed to whisper memories of Legna.

In the kitchen, a mug with half a cup of coffee sat on the table, next to a hardened sweet roll on a blue china plate. In the center of the table a glass vase held daisies, wilted, with the heads of the flowers bent down as if they were weeping. He then glanced at Legna's typewriter and thought he heard her pecking at the keys, sitting there and praying for the right words. His legs then led him to the bedroom where he took out the metal chest containing Legna's will and her memoir, her gift to Sammy. The memoir was inside a folder and held together with a thick rubber band. And it seemed odd to find Legna's memoir in the locked metal chest, among social security cards, birth certificates, and a curled marriage license.

When Sammy opened the envelope containing the will it read:

I, Legna Swinehauser, being of sound mind, leave my estate to my son, Sammy Swinehauser. The proceeds

of my trust fund, at the time of my death, will be
$200,000.

After reading the last sentence, Sammy had to read it again. He would be a wealthy man. Yet he found no joy in his new-found wealth; for no amount of money could buy a new soul.

Sammy placed the manuscript under his arm and went into the living room. Sitting down on the couch, he slipped the band from the manuscript and read the first page:

A Memoir ~ ~ ~ By Legna Swinehauser

Dedicated to my son, Sammy, a boy who is

like "A Sparrow in the Wind", who wants

only to sit on a branch and sing.

Sammy could feel a lump rise in his throat, and his palms were moist as he leafed through the pages.

He then remembered telling Legna how he always read the last part of a book first. Old habits never die, and as he began reading Legna's memoir, Sammy found himself turning to the end of the manuscript. She wrote: ~~

To wake up from a nightmare, you only have to open your eyes. But what happens when you open your eyes and the nightmare continues? What happens when the man you share your life with flies into a rage when you tell him Dr. Watkins will help him, give him medication to calm his mind.

But what really frightened me was when Max took the rifle down from above the fireplace and began carrying it through the house, aiming it at the picture on the mantel of Sammy and me. Then I knew what I had to do. I began carrying my pistol in my robe pocket or in my jeans. Anywhere I could reach for it to protect Sammy from Max.

Then one night after Sammy had gone to bed, Max stormed into the kitchen and demanded Sammy go back to St. Joseph's Home. "I want him out of my house," he hollered.

"Over my dead body," was all I could think to answer.

Max glared at me and narrowed his eyes. He then stomped out of the kitchen, cussing under his breath. But as I washed the dishes, I could hear him behind me, yet he didn't speak a word. When I did turn around, Max stood holding the Remington rifle with a wild look in his eyes.

"What's ... gotten into you? Maxim, Maxim, put the rifle down," I pleaded. "Please put the rifle down."

Even calling him "Maxim", as his mother had done, didn't calm him down. And with his teeth clenched, his words came out slow. 'First you and then the boy,' he said in a slow, methodical tone.

What happened next is a blur — something I've gone over and over in my mind. Max leveled the rifle, and the blast shattered the window behind me. And it was as if someone else had reached into the pocket of my robe and pulled out the pistol. The sound of that shot still echoes in my mind, the shot that pierced Max's chest. His rifle fell to the ground, and Max slumped to the floor. I ran over and knelt down beside him.

"Max," I sobbed, cradling him in my arms. "Why … did it have to come to this?" I did love you. Didn't matter if you loved me. Now … nothing matters."

But he couldn't answer, because Max was dead. Sobbing, I held him, rocked him, and all I could do was ask him why. Then the reality of what happened began to set in. Since Sammy was a heavy sleeper, he heard nothing. But if he wakened, how would I explain to him what I had done? How could I explain to anyone what I had done? If I called the police, would they believe me? Would there be a trial? Would they take me away, and would Sammy become an orphan again?

I paced around the kitchen, not believing what I had done and what I was about to do. All I could think of was Sammy, and I couldn't risk losing him. I then got the cart from the back porch, pulled it into the kitchen, and loaded Max's lifeless body into the cart. I then wheeled it down to the crematory.

As smoke billowed from the chimney, I prayed.
"Everything I did was to save Sammy. I never meant to
harm Max." Then the sobs came again and I asked
God to forgive me for what I was about to do.

It was midnight when the furnace stopped spewing
smoke into the night air. And it was as though someone
else was placing Max's ashes in the mason jar, and
someone else was walking out into the night. Only
when the wind brushed against my face did I realize
this was not a dream. Walking under a sky, lit by only a
few stars, I grabbed a cluster of marigolds from the
flower bed and went into the woods. With Max's ashes
in the jar, I emptied the ashes next to a sycamore tree.
Then, I took a stick, dug a hole and planted the
marigolds at the base of the tree. Kneeling down I
prayed, and the tears began to flow again. "My poor
Max. I did love you. We both let each other down, and
I'm so sorry." I hugged the tree, as if embracing Max
one last time, but when I turned around, I almost died
of fright. Otis, the man who prowled the woods at
night, stood beside me.

"Miss Legna, what'cha doin' out here? And why ya hugging a tree?" he asked, with chew tobacco dribbling from his mouth.

"Everything's fine, Otis. I ... was just going home."

I tried to keep my legs steady, my body from shaking, as I walked back to the house. But when I went inside, I faced the terror again. Glass from the broken window littered the kitchen floor, and blood splattered the doorway. On the floor, the rifle rested as a silent witness to the horror that happened tonight. I hung it back on the rack, swept up the glass, and mopped the floor. I found a roll of plastic and taped the broken window. Then I sat, curled into a ball, and wanted to scream — a shrill piercing scream. But with God as my witness, I had to protect Sammy. And I never meant to harm Max.

Please, God, forgive me. ~ ~ ~ ~ ~ ~

Sammy sat motionless and listened to his heart pound. Legna, the tender soul who liked to walk in the woods at night, cup fireflies in her hand and laugh when she released them, was asked to do something no mother should have to do — take a life to save her son. Holding Legna's manuscript tight to his chest, Sammy began to sob. And through his sobs, he prayed for God to forgive her.

Then clutching the manuscript, Sammy walked over to the fireplace. Striking a match, he watched the logs come to life. The flames danced across the wood and warmed the room as if Legna's arms were around him. Soothing him. Telling him everything would be all right. He then placed the stack of pages, the manuscript Legna wanted only *him* to read, on top of the fire. The flames turned orange, then red. And as a tongue of fire devoured Legna's memoir, only she and Sammy would know the secret buried in the ashes.

Sammy then paced around the room, trying to make sense of things which never made sense. But when he sat down on the couch, he could almost feel the spirit of Legna beside him. And as he sat in the quiet, Sammy began to understand the disappearance of Max — a disappearance that had been shrouded in mystery.

When the fire died out only ashes remained. Sammy took the poker; and as he stirred the black soot, he knew What's *done is done.* He then took the picture from the wall of Legna, as a child, wading through a sea of wildflowers. Placing the picture under his arm, he left the house.

Before getting into his car, Sammy turned and stared back at the white frame house, filled with memories of Legna, a woman who wanted only to protect him. As he gazed at the house, with gnarled branches knotted overhead like arms, a burden had been lifted. God had brought light into darkness.

Then Sammy began driving, leaving cornfields and the hills of White Chapel behind. When he reached the city, he parked and hurried toward the courthouse. The pro-life rally was still underway, and Sammy weaved through a group of protestors carrying signs. He searched the crowd, then he saw her wearing a beige jacket and high leather boots that molded to her legs. Sammy walked over to Beth, and with each step, he left the pain of his old life behind.

Beth's eyes widened when Sammy took the sign from her hands. Then turning the sign over, he pressed hard with a pen, writing jagged letters across the wood. When he handed the sign back to Beth, *I Love You* was written across the wood. Beth stared down at the sign, and her face seemed blank, expressionless. Sammy could feel his chest tighten, and it was as though his heart had stopped beating. But as he started to walk away, someone touched his arm. Then without saying a word, Beth reached up and held his face in her hands. When their lips met, all the fear and all the guilt he had known was lost in a kiss. No one spoke, and with people milling around them, he held Beth close.

Then a little girl with wisps of blonde hair and eyes, enormous and blue, wandered over and stared up at them. A mother, with two small children in tow, came and took the little girl's hand. "You shouldn't wander off like that," she said. The little girl gazed up at her mother, with neither a smile nor a frown, and holding onto her mother's hand, they disappeared into the crowd.

Sammy folded his arms back around Beth, and when he spoke, he leaned down and whispered in her ear. "That little girl ... she reminded me of the time I was putting a crib together at the shelter. I dreamed someday I would have a daughter who looked like her with blonde hair and big blue eyes. But I have so many dreams and there's so much I have to tell you."

"It all started with a dream. My mother was crying and told me she had to leave me. But I wasn't to worry because an angel would come to watch over me. That angel was Legna." Sammy paused and tried to steady his voice. "I know it's hard to believe, but I still have one more dream. That empty building on Second Street ... I'm going to buy it and call the restaurant *Legna's Place*. But there's something else"

"What is it?" Beth asked.

"You need more space at the shelter, and there are empty apartments in that building. The mothers and their babies could stay there. They could be together and be a family. Legna ... she would have wanted that."

When Beth looked up, tears filled her eyes. As Sammy held her close, under a sky of endless blue, Beth felt a warmth settle over them. Legna was looking down.

And she was smiling.

Though I am dead, grieve not for me.

I am so near, yet every tear you shed fills me with sorrow.

But when you laugh, my soul is lifted to the light.

So laugh and be glad for all life is giving, and I though dead

will share in your joy of living.

And on a day known only to God, we will meet again.

For we are all like "A Sparrow in the Wind."

~ ~ ~ ~ ~ ~ ~ ~

Made in the USA
Middletown, DE
15 September 2023